"Why do you have stars in your eyes, and why are you licking your lips like that?!"

Academy City Level Zero student
Touma Kamijou

"N-now's my chance!! I'll make it up to you with my body!!"

Member of New Light, a sorcerer's society reserve group in the United Kingdom
Lesser

A Certain Magical
Index
21

KAZUMA KAMACHI

ILLUSTRATION BY
KIYOTAKA HAIMURA

"Spill it.
Everything
you know."

Academy City
Level Five
Accelerator

"Accelerator…?!"

Former underling member of Item
Shiage Hamazura

"Is the Original not here on personal affairs herself? asks Misaka for confirmation."

Sister entrusted to an Academy City affiliate in Russia
Misaka number 10777

"…Well, it's not for business…"

Academy City
Tokiwadai
Middle School
Level Five
Mikoto Misaka

"nipsergNEXTnsig"
"sbrgNEXTsnmtph"
"nithgNEXTgbsvrfl"

Archangel who appeared in the skies of Russia
Gabriel (THE POWER OF GOD)

"Preparations complete. Commencing attack."

Nun managing the Index of Prohibited Books
Index

"That's...her remote-control Soul Arm!!"

English Puritan sorcerer from Necessarius
Stiyl Magnus

" ...... "

Archbishop of the English Puritan Church
Laura Stuart

"Misaka loves selfish plot developments like that. It's making her hard all over. ☆"

Clone of Misaka created in the
Sisters' Third Season
Misaka Worst

contents

VOLUME 21

KAZUMA KAMACHI

ILLUSTRATION BY: KIYOTAKA HAIMURA

NEW YORK

A CERTAIN MAGICAL INDEX, Volume 21
KAZUMA KAMACHI

Translation by Andrew Prowse
Cover art by Kiyotaka Haimura

TOARU MAJYUTSU NO INDEX Vol.21
©KAZUMA KAMACHI 2010
Edited by Dengeki Bunko
First published in Japan in 2010 by KADOKAWA CORPORATION, Tokyo.
English translation rights arranged with KADOKAWA CORPORATION, Tokyo, through Tuttle-Mori Agency, Inc., Tokyo.

English translation © 2019 by Yen Press, LLC

Yen On
150 West 30th Street, 19th Floor
New York, NY 10001

Visit us at yenpress.com
facebook.com/yenpress
twitter.com/yenpress
yenpress.tumblr.com
instagram.com/yenpress

First Yen On Edition: December 2019

Yen On is an imprint of Yen Press, LLC.
The Yen On name and logo are trademarks of Yen Press, LLC.

Library of Congress Cataloging-in-Publication Data

Names: Kamachi, Kazuma, author. | Haimura, Kiyotaka, 1973– illustrator. | Prowse, Andrew (Andrew R.), translator. | Hinton, Yoshito, translator.
Title: A certain magical index / Kazuma Kamachi ; illustration by Kiyotaka Haimura.
Other titles: To aru majyutsu no index. (Light novel). English
Description: First Yen On edition. | New York : Yen On, 2014–
Identifiers: LCCN 2014031047 (print) | ISBN 9780316339124 (v. 1 : pbk.) |
   ISBN 9780316259422 (v. 2 : pbk.) | ISBN 9780316340540 (v. 3 : pbk.) |
   ISBN 9780316340564 (v. 4 : pbk.) | ISBN 9780316340595 (v. 5 : pbk.) |
   ISBN 9780316340601 (v. 6 : pbk.) | ISBN 9780316272230 (v. 7 : pbk.) |
   ISBN 9780316359924 (v. 8 : pbk.) | ISBN 9780316359962 (v. 9 : pbk.) |
   ISBN 9780316359986 (v. 10 : pbk.) | ISBN 9780316360005 (v. 11 : pbk.) |
   ISBN 9780316360029 (v. 12 : pbk.) | ISBN 9780316442671 (v. 13 : pbk.) |
   ISBN 9780316442701 (v. 14 : pbk.) | ISBN 9780316442725 (v. 15 : pbk.) |
   ISBN 9780316442749 (v. 16 : pbk.) | ISBN 9780316474542 (v. 17 : pbk.) |
   ISBN 9780316474566 (v. 18 : pbk.) | ISBN 9781975357566 (v. 19 : pbk.) |
   ISBN 9781975331245 (v. 20 : pbk.) | ISBN 9781975331269 (v. 21 : pbk.)
Subjects: CYAC: Magic—Fiction. | Ability—Fiction. | Nuns—Fiction. | Japan—Fiction. | Science fiction. | BISAC: FICTION / Fantasy / General. | FICTION / Science Fiction / Adventure.
Classification: LCC PZ7.1.K215 Ce 2014 | DDC [Fic]—dc23
LC record available at https://lccn.loc.gov/2014031047

ISBNs: 978-1-9753-3126-9 (paperback)
978-1-9753-3127-6 (ebook)

1 3 5 7 9 10 8 6 4 2

LSC-C

Printed in the United States of America

COMBAT REPORT

World War III had finally begun.

On a flat-screen television, a female reporter could be seen standing at attention as she held her microphone with a solemn air, blizzards and smoke in the background.

"Eleven days have passed since fighting broke out. Even today, October 30, the flames of war near the Elizalina Alliance of Independent Nations border region show no signs of sputtering out!! Whoa—was that an Academy City bomber I just saw?! The Japanese government has repeatedly denied any intent of going to war, and this incident is believed to be Academy City acting on its—"

Civilians weren't the only ones in a panic. A female pilot of the Russian Air Force, engaged in live combat over the Sea of Japan, was gnashing her teeth, too.

"A minimal combat force for defense, my ass! They've got enough power to turn all of Russia into a sea of flames ten times over!!"

"This is Ryuuta Kameyama of the Academy City Air Defense Team... You can't run from the speed of light. I'll shoot you down real gentle, young lady, so get ready."

And at the war's epicenter, a spiky-haired boy named Touma Kamijou and a young sorceress named Lesser were walking through the white Russian snow.

"Fiamma again. He instigated this war with Academy City from behind the scenes in the Roman-Russian faction."

"Fiamma is on the sorcery side, through and through, but it doesn't seem like all he's aiming for is to mobilize the military. His timing for using the remote-control Soul Arm to access the Index's 103,000 grimoires bothers me, too."

"Whatever the case, there's only one thing to do: cave Fiamma's face in and save Index."

At the same time, near the border between Russia and the Elizalina Alliance of Independent Nations, Shiage Hamazura and Rikou Takitsubo were once again racing across a battlefield in a stolen car.

"Either way, we can't go on without Academy City's technology. Defeating the City can't be our goal."

"Hamazura, we have to look for something in this war to negotiate with. If we search for where the fighting is the thickest and pinpoint a spot where we can affect the direction of the war..."

Deep into Russian territory, aboard a transcontinental freight train, Accelerator was curled up, holding the nearly unconscious Last Order. After the appearance of Aiwass, a supernatural being, the little girl had sustained terrible damage due to the Misaka network's immense drain.

Accelerator, who had taken down the powered suit–clad group attacking the freight train, checked inside the trunk the assailants had been about to steal while remembering what Aiwass had said.

"Parchment, huh? Is this supposed to be the clue I need to save the kid?"

Kamijou and Lesser had arrived in the Elizalina Alliance of Independent Nations because the Alliance had secured the nun Sasha Kreutzev, a necessary piece in Fiamma's plans. The Alliance's aim was to ruin Fiamma's schemes. But when Fiamma appeared and effortlessly defeated both the sorceress Elizalina and Vento of the Front (who also happened to be present), he'd kidnapped Sasha.

As he departed, he'd said to Kamijou, "How will the 103,000

grimoires punish you when it realizes the truth? I'll be looking forward to seeing it."

Meanwhile, on a settlement close to the national border:

To aid Takitsubo, whose condition had suddenly worsened, Hamazura met a man named Digurv. Together, the two were led to a small settlement near the border with the Alliance, where Hamazura placed her in the care of its clinic. However, a hired team of foreign privateers affiliated with the Russian military abruptly attacked the settlement.

"What now? Run as far as we want—if they shoot us from the air, it's over. They'll kill us all!!"

"We'll use that anti-air gun. If we use the vehicle they left behind, we can take on the attack helicopters!!"

At a snowfield near a Russian Air Force base:

Accelerator and Last Order, crossing leagues of Russian snow before finally reaching the parchment's original destination, came under attack from Academy City. The assailant's identity was Misaka Worst. A somatic-cell clone from the Third Season, which shouldn't have existed.

"They decided how to deal with the problem. Kill everyone in the useless old series. And Misaka and the rest of the new series will update the network."

Within a conifer forest near the settlement:

Inside what was basically a half-destroyed anti-air cannon, Hamazura lay dumbfounded.

The attack helicopter that had been dancing through the skies had gotten skewered by a giant sword.

A rugged mercenary pulled the sword out of the shot-down helicopter's flaming wreckage.

"…Would you allow me, Acqua of the Back, to offer what assistance I may?"

On a road leading from the Russian border to a town:

Lesser, watching Touma Kamijou and Accelerator's battle, gulped audibly.

Accelerator's black wings split into countless pieces, attacking simultaneously from numerous directions; Kamijou, knowing he couldn't erase all the fragments with his right hand, had used Accelerator's against him, grabbing his black wings and twisting them.

However...

Does that really explain it on its own...?

Then, within the Elizalina Alliance of Independent Nations:

When the beaten Accelerator opened his eyes, he was in the bed of a truck. Near Last Order, who slept next to him, was a small note. In bad handwriting, it read:

Index Librorum Prohibitorum.

"The index of prohibited books..."

The war continued to swallow up ever greater numbers of people, changing spontaneously.

Confusion filled the comms between the fighter jets battling above the Sea of Japan.

"The Kremlin Report...?"

"A defensive procedure to deploy curtains of biological weapons around nuclear facilities. Kills only humans with a lethal virus so they can retake an unharmed facility. Now that they feel like they might lose the war, the Russian military is considering using it immediately. Without ordering nearby civilians to evacuate first."

The pope of Rome, who had been sleeping in a hospital in the Italian capital, slowly opened his eyes. He opened the hospital room's window, and as he got ready to sneak out, he magically established a line of communications with Vasilisa, a sorceress from the Russian Catholic Church.

"I've virtually no authority left. I cannot end this war with a single word."

"But you still made a stand and tried to stop it. Maybe you still have some value after all."

And in Academy City—

Two additional supersonic bombers were about to take off from

District 23 runways. In one rode Academy City's fourth-ranked Level Five, Shizuri Mugino.

Missing an arm and an eye, she was embarking on a hunt—and not for Russian soldiers.

"...I caaan't wait—can you, Haaamazuraaa?"

In the other bomber rode the third-ranked Level Five, Mikoto Misaka.

...After defeating everyone on the team tasked with the mission to take out Touma Kamijou—essentially all the people who were originally supposed to be in the plane.

"I'm this close to the end of my rope. If you don't get me to Russia soon, you'll be in a world of hurt."

On a base near the Russian border:

Fiamma of the Right, returning to his base, exchanged words with the Russian bishop Nikolai Tolstoj through magic.

"*Academy City's unmanned weaponry is overwhelming us. You were the one who convinced us to join this war— Do you understand how things will end if it keeps going like this?!*"

"Don't panic. The archangel Gabriel...Would that stop your sleep talk?"

...*Of course, I didn't get my hands on it for such a trivial purpose.*

An angel built under another set of rules, the aggregate of Academy City's AIM dispersion fields, Hyouka Kazakiri. She extended wings from her back and shot through the skies above the Sea of Japan.

She had one reason: to save her friend.

"Do not lay a hand on my friends, please...If you do, then I will be your enemy, even if we devour each other in the end."

In St. George's Cathedral in the UK capital, sorcerer Stiyl Magnus was trembling in anger. Before his eyes was a small figure, slowly rising, motions stiff and unnatural.

It was Index—the girl who had memorized and stored 103,000 grimoires inside her brain.

"Hostility, confirmed. Now...analyzing utilized spells, and... commencing construction of a corresponding Local Weapon..."

Fiamma of the Right was on the verge of attaining everything by taking advantage of the great war.

And so Touma Kamijou, heading for his base, muttered to himself.

"It's a good bet that I'm the worst kind of person for tricking Index. But the one I need to apologize to sure as hell ain't Fiamma of the Right."

CHAPTER 5

The Complex Game Board of the Battlefield
Enter_Project.

1

In a town blanketed by pure-white snow, several trucks had been parked in a row.

Inside one rode a spiky-haired boy named Touma Kamijou. Lesser, the young sorceress next to him, rummaged through a paper bag from a global fast-food chain, filling the vehicle with the aroma of meat and sauce. It was wartime, but apparently that hadn't affected the flow of goods yet.

As Kamijou tossed a nugget covered with a reddish sauce into his mouth, he said, "Gotta say, I never thought I'd be able to enjoy this flavor all the way out here in Russia. Although, they could have at least had a Russian-limited borscht burger or something on the menu."

"The convenience is all about the food tasting the same no matter where in the world you are. Rather useful when you can't handle the local cuisine."

Lesser spoke casually as she spotted the fries she wanted, but Kamijou was no frequent-flying international businessman. In fact, he'd actually been quite aggressive in his desire to try out Russian food.

But he also understood that they didn't have time to enjoy a leisurely meal right now.

Dipping a fry into the sauce Kamijou was holding, Lesser looked at him seriously and said, "We got this far by mixing in with smuggling brokers, but this is about as far as we'll get in a vehicle. The Russian base Fiamma's holing up in is about twenty-five miles away. Just like last time, we'll sneak inside with the underground train they use to bring things in."

"...Looks to me like we're going in from a different direction. I don't remember a town like this last time."

"They'd spot us in a flash if we used the exact same route. We even captured a Russian sorcerer at that station, remember?"

Seeming unhappy with just one fry, she shoved four or five in her mouth at a time like a gatling gun and munched them down.

"From hearing the slight accent in their voices, I can tell almost for certain that they mobilized all the sorcerers in this village. Which means we can assume there's another underground railway set up nearby, maybe in town."

"Is that how it works?"

"Yes. You always customize secret bases so you can use them easily. It's easy to make a maze or install all kinds of traps, but if it takes two or three hours to get through every time, it would slow down work. I can say that with confidence, since I've set up secret hideouts in Britain before."

"Huh," said Kamijou, tossing the last nugget into his mouth. "...What about the people Elizalina ordered to come with us in these trucks? What are they going to do?"

"You can think of them as something like a theater troupe that's pretending to be human smugglers for us. They have some military experience, but they can't stand up to frontline Russian soldiers, and they definitely can't do anything against professional Russian sorcerers. Their job is complete now that we're in this close. After this, they'll go back to the Alliance, pretending to have their 'guest' on board."

A complicated feeling welled up in Kamijou—he was more anxious now, but at the same time, he was relieved.

They were up against the top beast of the sorcery side: Fiamma of the Right.

There was no guarantee they'd win. Kamijou, a mere high school student, wanted as much combat power as he could get. On the other hand, he had trouble coming up with anyone who could contend with a monster like that. He couldn't bring himself to use anyone as a shield after they said they wanted to fight alongside him.

Speaking of which, that also went for Lesser, who was sitting next to him.

When he glanced over at her face, she shoved another salt-covered fry into her mouth, saying "Whaf's frong?"

"Nothing," he said to change the topic after she looked at him blankly. "Still—smuggling brokers, huh?"

"Oh, not familiar with the term? I would have thought Japan has quite a lot of them," Lesser replied casually as she swallowed her food.

"In most countries that share land borders with their neighbors, illegal immigration can be as easy as jumping over a fence in the night. Especially now that we're in the middle of a war. There's no end of people who want to leave the country, driven out by the dull roar of explosions and gunfire."

"…I didn't know that many people were flooding into the Alliance."

"It goes both ways," said Lesser aloofly. "It doesn't matter if Russia wins or Academy City wins—even a layman can tell it'll be over quickly. Nobody wants to end up being a citizen of a defeated nation. Fleeing abroad during times like that is a gamble. Your life will change massively depending on what side you're on when the war ends. If your prediction is wrong, you will have escaped a country only to be marked as a member of the losing one, so you'd have to be very careful…I hear there's even people who go back and forth between countries a bunch of times. Restless, like they're waiting for a game of musical chairs to end."

"…"

What a crappy state of affairs, thought Kamijou.

Those people moving from one nation to another weren't being forced to—they left their homes voluntarily, hoping to find a place where they could be happy. But lying at the bottom of that idea was anxiety and fear. Ordinarily, nobody would have had to abandon their homes or homelands.

Maybe everyone was like that.

Discarding things they didn't need to discard, things that shone so brightly, under the false assumption that they *wanted* to. Maybe that's what this huge war really was, too.

"We should put an end to it quick," said Lesser in a carefree tone, shoving her arm into the paper fast-food bag and fishing around. "Fiamma's the one pulling the strings behind the war anyway, right? If we beat him up, stop the fighting as soon as we can, return peace to the world, and get Britain some hefty reparations while we're at it, it'll be a perfect ending."

"…Yeah."

Though I'm not so sure about all that reparations stuff, added Kamijou to himself, mostly agreeing with Lesser's opinion. However it all shook out, it wouldn't change what he had to do.

"We'll smash Fiamma and rescue Index."

"Now that that's settled, let's wrap up this nutrient replenishment. With this triple!!"

"Hey, wait, that hamburger's as big as a vaulting horse. I don't think you can eat that without breaking it apart."

More specifically, it looked far too big to fit in the short Lesser's tiny mouth, but…

"Not to worry. I may look small, but I can fit things in my mouth that are so big everyone around me would be shocked—and I'm proud of it. You can take that in a somewhat lewd way if you want."

Spouting incomprehensible nonsense as always, Lesser chomped down onto the triple-decker burger. The huge serving of food began to fold in the middle and into her mouth.

And a moment later—

Squish!! Out of the opposite end of the hamburger she was biting into flew a chunk of ground beef that couldn't fit inside any longer. The juicy meat splattered on Kamijou's student uniform.

"…"

A moment's silence came.

Looking highly distraught, Kamijou glanced between his clothes and Lesser's face.

And then Lesser…

"N-now's my chance!! I'll make it up to you with my body!!"

"Why do you have stars in your eyes, and why are you licking your lips like that?! You aren't sorry at all, are you?!"

2

The roaring wouldn't stop.

At a spot about fifteen miles north of the Elizalina border, Russia's land and sky were both a sheer pane of white. And yet, unhealthy-looking black smoke was spurting up through the winter scenery.

Resting in the snow were a tank and an armored car, both resembling empty cans ground down by cogs. Other things lay scattered about—for example, chunks of concrete that were once standing walls and ceilings. This wreckage was the source of the smoke blotting out the pristine white vista.

Death.

That was what it smelled like to Shiage Hamazura.

And yet…the smoke wasn't from the nearby settlement.

It was from the privateers' garrison base.

The fortress, defended by top-of-the-line Russian equipment, had been swallowed in a vortex of destruction.

Obviously, Hamazura and the others couldn't have managed something like that.

The privateers had attacked the settlement twice, but that hadn't been all the troop power they could have mustered. In any case, more soldiers were on standby. The force they had in reserve probably numbered over five or even ten times that. Bases had a bare minimum number of personnel needed to continue running smoothly.

Then who was responsible?

The answer to that question came into view as Hamazura watched through a pair of binoculars he held in a tight grip.

Blue clothes.

A giant sword.

A tall man who called himself a mercenary.

Before this battle had started, Hamazura exchanged a few words with the man who had brought down an attack helicopter. But he still had no idea what was going on. A saint? Sorcery? The guy was acting like he hailed from a completely alien culture.

Hamazura had only learned a few things.

That the man called himself Acqua. That he had some kind of powers, different from esper abilities. Also, he was apparently on their side—and he would assault the base where the privateers were garrisoned.

It all seemed like a farce.

But…

…*Is this some kind of joke? I don't know what system his power's based on, but I don't know if even our Level Five espers could have made it such a one-sided fight.*

With every swing of his sword, huge swaths of snow melted into multi-ton masses of water that hurtled at the enemy tanks and armored cars. When a helicopter fired all its rockets at him, the man had answered with twice as many spears of ice, intercepting every single one of them. Soon after, when the water vapor in the middle of enemy lines burst outward in a sphere, the fortress, made of thick reinforced concrete, tore apart like a vinyl umbrella caught in a typhoon.

Supernatural phenomena; a natural disaster: That's exactly what this man's huge water attacks were.

Like a giant snake on the hunt, the liquid under his control floated in complete disregard for gravity and spanned dozens, if not hundreds, of meters. Just moments ago, Hamazura and the others had been engaged in a death match with the privateers. Now, it sent a chill down his spine as he watched a one-sided massacre unfold.

"What the hell...?" groaned Digurv, still in the anti-air tank with him. "Is that one of those supernaturals Academy City developed...?"

No, thought Hamazura.

But before he could mount any actual argument, the duel was over.

Except—it had never been a duel.

Destruction. Elimination. Eradication.

Those were the only words that could be sensibly used to describe the battle, which had lasted a scant twenty minutes.

"...I suppose that will do for now. However, this nation is incredibly large, and they will likely replenish their personnel quickly," said the mercenary in blue, sword on his shoulder, in a level voice.

Hamazura didn't know when the man had appeared. Just a moment ago, the guy had been standing somewhere Hamazura could only just barely make out through his binoculars.

The mercenary was far from out of breath—which was absurd considering how he'd supposedly just been fighting with his life on the line.

What the hell is this...?

Hamazura opened the vehicle's roof hatch and leaned out. He scowled immediately at the cutting chill and the stench of smoke, now several times thicker than earlier.

The tall man wearing blue gripped a giant sword in his hand. Its length alone was over three meters, and who knew how many hundreds of kilograms it weighed. No matter how anyone thought about it, that sword was too big for someone to hold in one hand.

Baffled, Hamazura muttered, "I'm gonna ask you again—what *are* you?"

"Acqua of the Back. A has-been mercenary and a thug."

He seemed to think he was replying to the question, but it didn't answer much. Hamazura still didn't understand anything—like how this man could summon such muscle power that clearly broke the limits of the human body, or even fundamental things, like what group he belonged to or who he was allied with.

Esper powers...?

Hamazura thought back to what Digurv had said moments ago.

He'd been living in Academy City until now, and he naturally tried to process this as the kind of "inexplicable phenomenon" he was used to seeing.

But this was different.

Even now, orbs of water floated about the tall man like he was in outer space, completely unaffected by gravity. They'd protected him from the heat, flames, and shock wave after he blew up the attack helicopter earlier.

Espers couldn't use more than one ability.

Is he controlling the moisture in his body to augment his muscle strength? No, human bodies are sensitive to changes in internal pressure. If he did that, his blood vessels and cells would just rupture. That doesn't explain it. Which means...

After thinking that far, Hamazura felt like he was about to be thrown into a new whirlwind of confusion.

Could it be?

Did this mean *something*, some unknown entity that transcended the normal rules of physics apart from Academy City's supernatural powers, really existed?

"Hamazura."

A voice called to him from inside the anti-air vehicle. It was Grickin, the Russian soldier who had fought alongside him. His face, pointed at Hamazura, was drawn with tension.

"This is bad...The radio picked up some transmissions. It's encoded, so I don't know what's being said, but the signal is getting steadily stronger."

"It's getting closer," said Digurv, riding in the same vehicle. "More privateer reinforcements?"

"Wait," Hamazura instructed, cutting him off. He'd just realized who the radio transmission was coming from.

He checked the binoculars to make sure. *Something* was near the white horizon.

There were over thirty tanks drawing closer that he could see, as well. They were on a different technological level than the mobile anti-air gun Hamazura was in; the designs were obviously different, but judging from the armor, these newcomers weren't even in the same league.

And the approaching force wasn't only tanks.

Advancing behind the cover of the lead tanks, he could see multiple foot soldiers wearing what looked like body armor made from composite materials. The armored cars without any visible guns running alongside the rest of the formation were probably supply vehicles for providing electricity to the force's various high-tech weapons. In the sky above them were tiny, remote-control aircraft buzzing about, each about a foot long. They seemed to be recon UAVs, but some of the models had thin tubes on their wings. Most likely, they were built for simple bombing runs, delivering the grenades attached to their dart-like tail ends by having them glide through the air.

This unit was clearly different from the privateers they had been seeing until now.

They'd brought more than one type of weaponry.

This was a formation designed for combat, using multiple varieties of soldier and weapon to cover one another's weaknesses. There wasn't a single hint of playfulness in their equipment. It left no openings to take advantage of, leaving Hamazura's hodgepodge team no chance of winning.

Hamazura gulped audibly and then offered, "They're not privateers…"

"What?"

Digurv frowned. Hamazura answered again.

*   *   *

"That's an Academy City military force."

Hamazura had kept his eyes on the infantry marching in the tanks' shadow. They wore armor-like gear, made from composite material—in other words, powered suits. Even Hamazura, a layman when it came to war machinery, could say one thing for sure: The only people who could put such things to practical use had to be from Academy City.

...*Looks like regular,* official *soldiers. They don't seem to have any connection to the underworld like us,* guessed Hamazura offhandedly.

Of course, there was a possibility that people from that underworld were simply using normal Academy City equipment—but he rejected that idea, not with knowledge but intuition. People from the underworld like Hamazura would never strut around so openly. Even if they tried to behave that way, their "scent" would always be detectable.

"It seems as though they've come to occupy this place," said Acqua flatly, giant sword still on his shoulder. "What now? Shall I scatter them?"

"...No. I don't know if it lines up with your goals, but if we want to keep protecting that settlement, we better not resist now." Hamazura shook his head. "I don't know who you are or where you're from, but I know you're a monster. A monster on a level that even someone like me, who's lived in Academy City, can't figure out how you work. That means it would be better to purposely let Academy City's military garrison come here. They'll occupy the area for the moment, but they'll be able to protect it for months. Even if the privateers call up additional troops, these guys can deal with them. If we lash out without thinking, it won't help the settlement's situation."

"..." Acqua grunted and nodded slightly. He seemed to have accepted Hamazura's viewpoint.

"But...wait," said Digurv instead. "Hamazura, aren't you on the run from Academy City?"

The question gave Hamazura pause for a moment.

But only for a few seconds.

"…What can I do?"

Academy City's temperament, while not as bad as the privateers', would still be difficult to deal with. Hamazura knew that much—he'd fled from them, after all. But at the very least, they'd serve as a bulwark to protect the villagers from Russian tyranny—particularly that of the privateers.

The settlement had been a nice, comforting place. Despite Takitsubo's sudden arrival, everyone had worried about her condition. But neither Hamazura nor Takitsubo could afford to be caught here by Academy City. They absolutely couldn't let that happen until they found a means to negotiate.

The only thing they could do was run.

Flee the settlement that Hamazura had personally risked his life to protect.

"I don't think they know I'm here. But if they use their advanced sensors to search the area, they're more than likely to find us. Chances are slim that students have been mobilized, but if they had a psychometer or something, they'd catch us right away. I don't want any of you to hide information about us. Tell them everything that happened here. Don't do anything that might make those troops suspicious. If you keep a cooperative attitude, Academy City will protect you."

As he spoke, Hamazura internally reviewed his ideas.

"Of course, Academy City troops aren't allies of justice. They're just a combat force, a different kind than Russia's. But they'll do their best to take care of useful people who side with them. So if you give them information on us, you can take advantage of them, too."

"That's absurd," said Digurv quietly, though his voice trembled with anger. "Do you think we, for mere convenience, would abandon someone who fought alongside us?"

"Then what will you do? We don't know when the privateers will get reinforcements. It might be tomorrow, it might be in a week.

They might have a hundred people, and they might have a thousand. Are you saying you can fight them all off alone? That's unrealistic, no matter how you look at it."

"…But…"

"I don't plan to cut my life short at this age, and I don't feel like demanding that from any of you, either. I'll survive—just you watch. I'll flee to the ends of the earth to make sure of it."

As Hamazura spoke, he reached out and rapped his hand on the beaten-up anti-air vehicle's armor.

"Just this once, have faith in me. Don't give up so easy. What we carry isn't cheap—it's not something you can just throw away using the word *war* as an excuse."

The words *I'm sorry* played across the faces of the men by the mobile anti-aircraft gun.

But they kept it to themselves, so Hamazura decided he hadn't noticed. Digurv and Grickin had no reason to apologize.

He met Acqua of the Back's eyes. "I forgot to say something."

"What is it?"

"I wanted to tell you 'thanks.' Nobody needed to die—not me, not the settlement, not the woman I'm in love with—because you were here…I'll repay you someday."

He didn't have time to wait for an answer. Academy City's forces would occupy that settlement in the near future, then cut off all communications with the surrounding area. He had to get Takitsubo from the settlement and leave this region before that.

After parting with Acqua and driving the anti-aircraft vehicle close to the settlement, he got out of the steel chassis and ran across the deep snow. The residents wouldn't be in the destroyed buildings. Hamazura and the other fighters had made them evacuate their homes and take shelter in the southern woods. Hamazura hurried in that direction.

He felt like something invisible was weighing down on his back. Along the way, he tripped several times, rolling onto the snow as he desperately headed for the woods.

When he reached his goal, he heard several noises—hushed breathing. Faces were visible behind the trees here and there. The settlers. When they realized the person who had barged into the woods was Hamazura, they hastily rushed out from their hiding places. Someone shouted something in Russian, and a mother came to him with a small child at her side. She was holding an exhausted Rikou Takitsubo.

"Are you okay, Takitsubo?"

"The same goes for you, Hamazura—I'm so glad you're alive."

"Sorry. Things are getting dicey again."

After learning the situation, Takitsubo spoke slowly and calmly, despite a sweat-covered frown appearing on her face. "…The Elizalina Alliance of Independent Nations."

"What?"

"Academy City is steadily taking over Russian territory. At this rate, we'll never be able to run or hide from Academy City garrisons and their patrols. But if we cross the border, they won't have a pretext to come after us."

She was right—Russia apparently shared a nearby border with the Elizalina Alliance of Independent Nations. If it was a land border, the security probably wouldn't be that tight, either. All that was left was to figure out a way to break through. They'd cross the border temporarily to evade the Academy City's pursuit for the moment, then go back into Russian lands and resume their search for something they could use as a negotiation tool.

Now that they had a plan, they couldn't dally forever.

Lifting Takitsubo, who couldn't walk properly, onto his back, Hamazura was about to start trekking over the snow once again. How many miles was it to the border? How many dozens of miles?

And then someone from the settlement—a short old man—tossed something silver and shiny at Hamazura.

In confusion, he grabbed it; it was a car key.

The old man smiled and said something in Russian. Takitsubo translated.

"He says it's for a blue jeep parked outside the settlement."

"No, I couldn't." Hamazura was upset. "Academy City will probably come after us. If I take this, it'll make it look like someone from the settlement might have aided our escape. If that happens, we can't be sure their troops will protect you."

After he raised that point, the old man said something else in Russian.

According to Takitsubo: "He says to just turn on the engine without using the key. He wants it to look like you stole it without asking."

"Now that's something. What are you gonna do if they're listening in on this conversation with high-performance microphones or telepaths?"

Still, Hamazura and Takitsubo were up against military vehicles and powered suits. It would be impossible to outrun them if he had to carry someone limp on his back while walking through the deep snow.

He gave the key back to the old man, but it seemed like a better idea to accept his goodwill and "steal" the jeep.

When Hamazura began walking from the woods toward the settlement, many pairs of eyes saw him off. The little girl tried to grab Hamazura's clothes, but her mother stopped her. It was the same mother and daughter that the privateer anti-air vehicle had been chasing.

Readjusting Takitsubo on his back and hurrying ahead as if to shake them off, he muttered, "...I feel pathetic. The best choice I can come up with is to abandon them without trying."

"It's okay, Hamazura," answered Takitsubo, still hanging limp, bringing her mouth close to his ear. "You're still fighting to protect me. You're not pathetic."

As though spurred on by her words, Hamazura continued to run.

Their current destination was the Elizalina Alliance.

And to escape pursuit from Academy City's heavy armaments, first they'd need to get their hands on that jeep.

3

It was a small room made of stone, in a building that must have been some kind of fortress originally.

The sight of a building centuries old and still in use without seeing much preservation work may have seemed strange for Japanese people, whose dwellings were often built with wood in a part of the world that experienced frequent earthquakes. But indeed, the only updates that stood out in this place were necessities added afterward, like fluorescent lighting and air-conditioning.

Founded several years ago, the Elizalina Alliance of Independent Nations was a new up-and-coming country. Therefore, World War III—that massive change in the global status quo—had broken out before they'd built any modern military facilities, and so they seemed to have hurriedly incorporated military equipment like radars into existing infrastructure to transform them into makeshift army bases.

This old fortress was one of those facilities. Many of the men and women going between one door and the next were dressed in crude camouflage gear.

Amid them all stood Accelerator.

He had lost to the Level Zero but after he had been left unconscious in the Russian snow following their battle, he was brought to the Elizalina Alliance of Independent Nations thanks to that boy—it seemed he'd talked to them and gotten him transferred into their soldiers' care.

"How's my battery? …That good, huh…"

Accelerator raised a hand to the electrode on his neck.

The battery had been drained after several back-to-back fights, but now that he'd obtained a temporary resting place, he'd been blessed with a chance to recharge it. The voltage, current, and plug shape were all different from Japan's, so he couldn't simply use the devices he had on hand. Instead, he'd successfully dismantled a local adapter and adjusted the insides.

Back to his usual condition, Accelerator spread dozens of parchment sheets out on a wooden table.

They were the cargo the Russian forces had been trying to transport on that freight train. Scrawled all over them were occult patterns and handwritten incantations, the kind that wouldn't be out of place in a horror film. He could tell that each of the drawings was done by hand using sticky, waxlike ink. Despite the analog method, however, they were all exceedingly precise. The letters were uniform Latin script, but notes had been added here and there in small Russian characters.

He couldn't tell exactly what it said. He didn't even know whether it had any real meaning.

However:

...It seems like some kind of instruction manual. I can tell the pictures here are done in sequence, like it's following steps for something, but...

Accelerator's eyes shifted, glancing around until he found a Caucasian man wearing a dirt-cheap camo outfit staring at the parchment with a somehow meek expression. The fluorescent lights, clashing with the centuries-old stone building, made the soldier's skin appear even paler.

Accelerator asked in Russian, "Do you know what this is?"

Despite making the effort to speak his language, though, the soldier's shoulders gave a jerk. He seemed to be simply afraid, in addition to being surprised that Accelerator had suddenly addressed him in Russian.

The soldier gave Accelerator a hard look up and down. "...You're Japanese, right?"

In response, the white-haired, red-eyed monster returned a casual glance and answered the question with another one. "What do I look like?"

The soldier must have spotted the dangerous irritation behind his eyes, and Accelerator was fairly confident that the man wouldn't be steering the conversation any further off topic. To help the idea along, Accelerator pointed to the parchment again and repeated, "Do you know what this is?"

"No..." The soldier shook his head. "But it looks like some kind of list of magical conversion requirements. I think it's giving directions on how to cast Roman Orthodox spells with Russian Catholic standards, explaining what to replace and how to replace them. But I can't tell what kind of spell, exactly, it's trying to communicate."

"..."

Accelerator assumed a dubious look, but the soldier shook his head, face paling, seeming to imply that he shouldn't expect any more than that. As several other soldiers bustled about, only Accelerator was still as they conversed.

The soldier continued. "Don't make that face. Unlike Lady Elizalina, I'm not up to snuff in this department. I've only gotten glimpses of it sometimes while on her personal security detail—I haven't studied it. If I could chant a spell and make a flame appear in my hand, I mean...I wouldn't be carrying around these hand grenades here, would I?"

He seemed to be under the false assumption that he'd offended Accelerator for not being able to provide the answer he was looking for, but that wasn't why Accelerator was currently frowning.

What the hell was this soldier *talking* about?

Magic? Spells? List of conversion requirements? Roman Orthodox? Russian Catholic? Activation methods? Department? Gotten glimpses? Study? Chant a spell and make fire in your hand?

The words flowed from the soldier's lips like they were the most natural thing in the world—and every last bit of it was beyond Accelerator's understanding. It wasn't a simple deception the man had thought up on the spot. Nor was it spiritualism or a religious take on things. The soldier had just rattled off nonsensical vocabulary as *realistically viable techniques*. He could tell by the man's tone of voice. It was no different from what someone would sound like if they were explaining the timing of when to pour wine into the pot as the secret ingredient to a meat dish.

He couldn't wrap his head around it.

But if there was anything that Academy City's number-one monster, the crystallization of scientific technology, couldn't understand...

Then maybe it was the key to solving the Last Order issue that had thoroughly stumped him so far.

The words Aiwass had given him: *Go to Russia*.

The note the Level Zero had left for him: *Index Librorum Prohibitorum*.

The key that would draw a straight line between them:

"...Who is Elizalina?"

"A sorceress—or no, rather, a wizard, I believe. That's apparently what they call casters who prefer to adopt disciples rather than work by themselves. I bet if the English Puritan Church, for example, knew about that, they'd sic some ferocious hounds on her. Lady Elizalina realigned the religious underpinnings of the Alliance and successfully raised and produced sorcerers for real combat. I mean, the Russian Church is one of the three largest religions in the world. It would be crazy to fight them head-on, but she can at least fling invisible spells from afar to maintain a defensive line. Which is the bare minimum requirement to call yourself a historical nation with a mature spiritual culture."

It would be easier to understand programming language at this point, thought Accelerator. The cultural differences were already well beyond what he could grasp in a few words.

"Anyway, this Elizalina chick—she can decode this parchment?"

"If she could talk." The soldier sighed. "She's in a field hospital bed at the moment."

"Great. I have no idea why I got brought to a place like this, and now my last resort for explaining shit is groaning in the hospital."

"Is your companion all right?"

The soldier was referring to Last Order.

The girl, who appeared to be about ten, lay sleeping on a sofa along the wall of the room they were in. Her body was limp against the cushions, and she didn't move a muscle. She had fully lost consciousness. Every time Accelerator remembered that he couldn't feel the "presence" of a person from her, the silence gave him a faint chill.

"Does she *look* all right? We had to flee the country for her."

"All the more reason you shouldn't move her." The Caucasian soldier looked between Accelerator and Last Order. "Whatever you want to do now, you can't keep bringing her along with you, can you? I mean, our hospitals might not be comparable to Academy City's cutting-edge technology, but maybe you should get her to one. Just having a bed can make a big difference."

"...I didn't plan on staying long or getting into bloodbaths anyway. Ideally, I'd like for this to be our goal line, with me solving everything ASAP here and now, then have that stupid kid throw one of her usual annoying tantrums."

As Accelerator scratched his head, he seemed to remember something else and asked, "Is there anyone besides Elizalina who can decipher this parchment?"

"...The sorcerers who belong to our unit have only gotten training for actual combat, so they can be unfamiliar with more orthodox concepts. I doubt you'll find anyone aside from Lady Elizalina who could do decoding on this level."

Which meant he'd just have to wait for the injured woman to wake up after all.

He had the choice of leaving the Alliance and searching for other leads, but like this soldier had said, Last Order's health was unpredictable. She wasn't in a state where he could drag her around without a concrete destination in mind.

...It's in my best interest, but I never thought I'd be keeping my schedule open for someone else.

"When's the sleeping beauty gonna wake up?"

"If all goes well, in one to three hours. That's when the general anesthesia wears off...But she *did* just have surgery. At most, she'll give the letters a look over. She needs absolute rest, and ordinarily, we'd want you to stay away from her."

"I see."

"What about the girl? If you need a bed, say so soon. You just crossed the Eurasian mainland—you know what state the world is in right now. We're at war. No guarantee those beds will stay open forever."

"…Yeah, I'd have to be an absolute moron to go into battle with a kid on my back. Considering her health, it might be better to toss her in a hospital or something.

"But—," added Accelerator.

Ba-bang-bang-bang!!

He abruptly took the gun out of his belt and shot through another nearby soldier's feet.

The man he'd just been speaking with froze up, sputtering.

In the meantime, Accelerator shot the feet of a few other men and women in the room.

"Spies," said Accelerator lazily. "If I'm gonna leave the kid to you, I need to make sure her environment is clean as can be."

Accelerator prodded one of the fallen, immobilized men with a foot. A small microphone and a recording-transmitting device, like the kind celebrities would use, was revealed to be connected inside his clothing via cable. The spies had been monitoring Alliance troop movements and transmitting it to Russia from here. Another possibility was that they'd been feeding poor advice or false information to distract Alliance forces.

His attendant soldier hurried to search the other wounded. Like the first, they all were carrying similarly hidden devices.

"These communicators don't reach far. There must be a communications officer with real equipment somewhere outside."

"Naturally, they're preparing to run away now that we noticed. Or maybe they'll try something more *for the motherland*, knowing they'll die in the attempt." Accelerator headed for the room's exit on his crutch. "In exchange for lodging, I'll mop these guys up for you. I don't have time to clean out the entire Alliance, all two hundred miles from east to west, but I'll exterminate all the pests in and around this sector. While I'm at it, I'll give you a lecture on how to tell which pests are harmful. Then you can handle it yourself."

"How did you know? Spies come in two flavors. The first shows their strength by organizing into a large-scale group, like the KGB or the CIA. The second doesn't maintain a name or structured organization—they take all the jobs that would cause international problems if things got into the public record. These people are clearly the second kind. Some teenager from Japan shouldn't be able to spot them."

"Not necessarily," Accelerator replied easily. "If you observe everyone's subtle traits and habits, you'll naturally find the ones who stand out against everyone else."

His words were delivered in such a light tone, so conversational, that it made the soldier shudder.

"This place you're all standing in now ain't the only hell out there. If you ask me, darkness in these parts is barely scratching the tip of the iceberg."

It was instantly obvious whether the intimation was a bluff or not.

And thus, the monster born of the world's most advanced technology and shaped by the greatest evil, who had been single-mindedly eradicating the darkness, began laying the necessary groundwork.

4

St. George's Cathedral, London.

"Chapter eight, verse twenty-five. Commencing elimination of entity obstructing remote access operation. Reverse-engineering spell structure of hostile entity."

A girl's voice flowed out smoothly.

The damaged record–like noise from just moments before had ceased.

And.

Roar!! Accompanied by an immense gust of wind, red wings sprouted from the young nun in white. They were a hue closer to that of blood than flames; and as intricate magic circles blinked in and out of existence in her pupils, she slowly turned her head, observing.

Index.

Seeing her utterly changed form, Stiyl Magnus scowled slightly. He never made a face when burning enemy sorcerers to a crisp, but he had wrinkles on his brow now, as though he was suppressing some pain.

"OOTFECOTW, TGFOB. (One of the five elemental components of the world, the great fire of beginning.)"

And yet, Stiyl didn't hesitate to fight.

He'd been entrusted with her life.

He took out a rune card.

"IITBLNL, AIITLOJTPTW. (It is the blessed light nurturing life, and it is the light of judgment to punish the wicked.)

"IFWGH, AIINMWECD. (It fills with gentle happiness, and it is numbing misfortune which extinguishes cold darkness.)

"IINF—IIMS. (It is named fire—it is my sword.)

"MTAMMBFGP!! (Manifest thyself and masticate my body for great power!!)"

No, it wasn't only one card. In an instant, a multitudes of cards were plastered on every single spot in the room. Too many—it was unearthly.

Flames roared to life.

A column of fire over ten feet tall appeared, coalescing into a human form. The fiery 3,000 degrees Celsius mass was named Innocentius—the Witch-Hunter King.

Index's head jerked slightly and took aim at her target.

A moment later.

Boom!!!!!!

By the time he heard the tremendous boom ring out, Innocentius had already been mowed down.

*   *   *

The red wings sprouting from the girl's back had swung around. That simple motion instantly tore through the blazing titan, supposedly supported by thousands of rune cards. It had even prevented automatic regeneration that should have activated. Due to feedback from the damage Innocentius had sustained, the cards surrounding it blackened, now useless.

This was ultimate defense system of the library of magical grimoires—the index of prohibited books that freely wielded the power of 103,000 volumes to protect the storehouse of knowledge from all would-be thieves.

However, Stiyl didn't have the time to calmly mull this over.

The defeated Innocentius fell apart and scattered in all directions, and the shock wave now bared its fangs at the flame's summoner.

"...?!"

Stiyl was thrown directly into the wall.

His back took the brunt of the impact, knocking the wind out of him. The girl, magic circles floating within her eyes, watched him calmly.

"Chapter ten, verse three. Confirmed effectiveness of current spell. Increasing spell's power and scope. Determining most effective method to terminate hostile entity's life-sustaining processes."

Foom!! Several red wings extended all at once.

Now extending far enough to scrape against the cathedral's ceiling, they assailed Stiyl with all the force of a steel trap slamming shut.

He had no time to think of a spell.

Willing his body to move despite nearly having lost its strength from the earlier blow, he rolled to the floor.

The many wings fell.

Only good fortune was responsible for none of them landing a direct hit.

However...

Following a great rumble, the floor of St. George's Cathedral split wide open.

It swallowed both Stiyl Magnus and the stone he stood upon, dropping them underground.

The very idea of breaking his fall somehow was nonexistent.

Every breath was accompanied by the taste of blood.

Stiyl had fallen faceup, and it took him a few moments to finally realize what had happened .

This was the basement's Soul Arm storehouse.

Index's attack had damaged the foundation itself, the backbone of the cathedral's structure.

Guh...hah...! Blast, how many barriers do you think we had set up? This cathedral is the main base of anti-sorcery operations—how could she break through it all in one attack...?!

Index's original purpose was to serve as a defensive mechanism to keep important technology and knowledge from passing into the hands of international magic societies.

Even ten thousand versus one wouldn't be enough to challenge her.

One versus one was the height of folly.

Fighting against her in her John's Pen state was the same as engaging in a full-scale war.

There was a time when a saint named Kaori Kanzaki was around. Once, there had been an illusion killer named Touma Kamijou.

But now, things were different.

He couldn't rely on those irregulars.

Then, he heard a scraping noise coming from above.

Stiyl peered up, still lying on his back, and saw the girl staring down at him from the edge of the collapsed hole.

Her lips—were moving.

"Chapter eleven, verse two. Confirmed effective destructive power. Determining optimal course of action—follow up with continuous attacks to deny opportunity to recover."

The library of grimoires jumped down from the crag-like height without hesitation.

Stiyl rolled to the side with all his might.

A moment later, Index's feet ruthlessly destroyed the spot where he had been lying.

5

He was pressing the accelerator so hard he thought it might break.

Turning the jeep's steering wheel with small, jerky motions, Shiage Hamazura desperately tried to keep the car tires from losing their grip on the snow. It had studded tires, which was forbidden in Japan, but on thicker snow like they were on now, the car was still about to slide sideways.

What was the reason he chose to drive so dangerously?

The reason was visible in his rearview mirror.

"Shit!! I can't even find a chance to shake them!!" he shouted, clenching his teeth.

Behind him, closing in from a distance of a little over 50 meters, were Academy City–made powered suits. The monsters came in a set of five like the main cast of a sentai superhero team, using the high speed of their suits to draw ever closer. Their pursuers slid across the ground with the ease of ice skates and leaped like they were participating in a triple jump event. These guys were keeping up on foot and steadily closing in.

Hamazura hadn't been able to get out of the encirclement safely. The enemy had troops to spare. Five foot soldiers should be more than enough to handle a single jeep was probably what they were thinking. They were clearly making light of him.

Still, under no circumstances was Hamazura about to provoke them. Fighting even one of those things head-on would end in instant death. A battle against five of them at once wouldn't last one-fifth of a second. Hamazura didn't even have the vocabulary to express it properly.

Takitsubo, securely buckled into the passenger's seat, looked up from the map on her lap and said, "Hamazura, they're closing in little by little."

"I know that!! Those bastards, coming after us like pro ice skaters or something!! With all that insane tech on full display, we're gonna have way more urban legends on our hands soon!!"

"It's about five hundred meters until the border with Elizalina. Can you make it?"

He didn't have time to answer.

The four-wheel-drive jeep had been just barely maintaining its balance, but now it was finally beginning to slide sideways. Hamazura hastily turned the wheel in an attempt to recover, but the car veered way off the road—which had no fence or guardrails—plunging into a forest of conifer trees.

Hamazura didn't have time to hit the brakes.

If he didn't keep the accelerator floored, the powered suits would catch them.

The scenery change came with an immediate uptick in sensory speed.

Trees thicker than power poles kept almost grazing the jeep as they passed at breakneck speeds.

Five hundred meters...

The powered suits wouldn't care.

Despite entering the forest at the same speed as Hamazura and Takitsubo, they continued their pursuit without hesitation, as though running across roller coaster rails. The snow-covered ground posed no problem—and sometimes they'd even kick down branches, boughs, and trunks to take bold shortcuts. Their strength hadn't simply been amplified with the machines. Their sensors and devices for heightening the speed of their decision-making abilities were out of this world. Maybe they had electrodes plugged directly into their brains.

Five hundred meters!!

And then the jeep was suddenly floating.

Inside the forest, the ground wasn't flat like asphalt.

The jeep had bounced off a slightly inclined bump, launching it up into the air like a jumping platform.

"Oh…sh—?!"

Before he could finish talking, the tires landed on the ground again.

The vehicle began sliding around incomparably more than before. Hamazura desperately manipulated the steering wheel, but in the blink of an eye, they'd ended up spinning ninety degrees sideways.

Still, luck was on their side.

A moment later, the car burst out of the forest and onto a snowfield.

And at the other side: the Elizalina Alliance of Independent Nations' border.

A chain-link fence, about two meters tall and topped with barbed wire, stood between the two nations, but Hamazura had already stopped thinking about it. If he was careless in trying to regain control over the jeep, he'd lose that much more time. Instead…

I'm gonna slide right in!!

They plunged toward it, still going sideways.

The powered suits' thick fingertips came close enough to reach out toward them, but all they grabbed was air.

An instant later, the metal fence wrapped around the jeep, and the driver's side window shattered with a brilliant noise. The jeep continued on, hurtling into Alliance territory; a strange sound rang out, almost like the front wheels had had gotten jammed up by what remained of the fence. As soon as Hamazura had that thought, the jeep finally lost what semblance of balance it had left. It continued to spin around and around three more times before ultimately coming to a stop with its front facing the Russian border.

They'd escaped.

It was only about twenty meters, but the jeep had definitely made it into Alliance. The justification for the presence of the powered suits—or rather, Academy City—in this war was only to fight Russia. They couldn't act freely within the borders of the Independent Nations.

However.

"You've gotta be kidding me...," moaned Hamazura from the driver's seat.

The powered suits couldn't lay a hand on them now—but they were still relentlessly coming closer.

They had to be aware of the border.

They knew, and they were ignoring it.

Nestled in their mechanical fingers were certain objects.

Insanely huge revolvers. The muzzles were so big a soda can could fit inside them. They probably shot grenades or something. What if they were actually oversize shotgun shells? How much power could each round possibly have? *Either way, this jeep ain't bulletproof, so one shot is all it'll take to turn into a ball of flames.*

The suits wasted no time aiming at them.

No voices to threaten them or give them a warning.

Hamazura immediately glanced at the driver's side door handle, but outside was covered in broken fence fragments; even if he tried to open it, it was staying right where it was.

I'd forgotten, he thought, staring at the muzzles blankly like they were tunnels connecting to death.

This wasn't a sporting event.

This wasn't a card game.

It was actual combat.

Hamazura had fled through countless back alleys in the City— didn't he know best that nobody would step in to referee if a weakling or loser cried foul?

He didn't even notice his mouth drying out.

The powered suits' thick fingers, riding on the giant revolvers' triggers, moved.

And then—

Hamazura heard a noise like fireworks going off. Not the bang when they exploded—it was the sound of the firework itself shooting up high into the sky from the ground.

He frowned.

There was no time to see where it was coming from.

Because a moment later…

Fwoosh!!
The national border transformed into a straight-edged sea of fire, engulfing the powered suits.

The scene looked like a joke.
The blast hadn't flown off in every direction like it should have. The flames spread unnaturally, like someone had poured oil on the ground in a line. Their height was about ten meters, and the length reached a good five-hundred. The jeep's front windshield shattered to pieces. A fair bit of distance separated them from the epicenter, but the intense light and heat blew straight into Hamazura's and Takitsubo's faces. The jeep itself, which had come to a stop in the snow, seemed like it slid a few centimeters when the shock wave passed.
"Wh…what?" squawked Hamazura, confirming that he could still use his own voice. "Napalm…?"
"Based on the sound we heard right before it…They must have been rockets loaded with liquid explosives."
Takitsubo seemed like she was barely breathing.
But she was still alive.
He didn't know who was responsible, but for the moment, he figured they should get out of the car now that it was unusable and take refuge inside the Elizalina Alliance of Independent Nations. However…
Bam!!
It was the sound of crumpling metal.
Someone was standing on the jeep's hood. It was unbelievable, but the person appeared to have fallen right out of the sky and landed there.
From the driver's seat, Hamazura could only see slender legs.
Since the person's heels were facing them, their face must have been looking toward the wall of liquid flames, where several powered suits writhed.

Despite the raging inferno, they were still operating properly. However, when they saw the person standing on the hood, they edged...away. A moment before that, though, Hamazura had seen them pause for just an instant. And then, as though withdrawing deeper into the wall of flames, the powered suits began to retreat.

The person on the hood seemed to have rescued Hamazura and Takitsubo from their crisis. But who was it?

The answer came a moment later.

Their apparent savior, who still had their heels facing them, used one of those heels to lightly tug on the broken windshield's frame. At least, that was what it looked like. But the simple gesture tore the jeep's roof off with a loud *riiiip*, completely separating it from the vehicle.

Grrk-grraaa!! came the tremendous noise as the view from the interior expanded all at once.

And dominating that new view: a monster with white hair and red eyes.

Shiage Hamazura knew who this was.

The monster's identity:

"Accelerator...?!"

"Great. Looks like my search for nearby spies got me caught up in some extra bullshit."

The monster spoke as though he found all this truly annoying.

"Spill it. Everything you know."

6

"You have me at a loss."

In a field hospital—well, in a stone fortress that had been around for centuries, a building that the staff had simply wheeled medical equipment into—a blond-haired, blue-eyed woman spoke in Japanese.

The woman, sitting up in bed, had bandages wrapped around various spots. But even disregarding them, she didn't appear physically fit. Her skin was more wan than fair, she sported large rings under her eyes, and her body was more bony than it was slim. On the whole, she was the kind of person who might have been beautiful if someone made her go on a sumo wrestler's diet for half a year straight.

Elizalina.

In a melancholic manner, the woman after whom the Alliance was named held her slender hands to her head.

"…If there was even a chance to use recovery magic, I'd like to do something about myself first in this situation."

"Ahhh. Uh, sorry."

"No need to apologize. I'm the one who claimed I didn't need to rest, and that only resulted in my aide needing to perform emergency surgery on me."

She seemed to be wounded in her own right, but it sounded like she'd treat Takitsubo. Mentally thanking her, Hamazura was still confused.

What was *re-coverie majik* supposed to be?

For a moment, he thought she'd learned some sort of incorrect Japanese, but Elizalina clearly had a better command of the language than the idiot Hamazura. If he took her words at face value, then…what did that mean, exactly?

Without thinking, he glanced over at Accelerator, who clicked his tongue at him and looked away.

Hamazura'd heard that the Independent Nations might have some kind of special medical technology that Academy City didn't. He didn't know whether it could alleviate Takitsubo's symptoms, but he'd figured that it would be worth asking. That was why he'd carried the limp young woman on his back to this field hospital, and yet…

Recovery? Recovery magic— Am I hearing that right? Like in RPGs? Or is it related to medicine somehow…Like convalescence? But wait, what about "magic"? Is that a medical term around here?

More question marks were popping up in his mind by the second, but he didn't ask them immediately because Elizalina had talked about it so fluidly and naturally. It could have been a con, but with all the words coming one after another without giving him a chance to interrupt, it made him feel like there had to be some kind of logic behind it.

Elizalina ignored him and turned her head.

Elizalina glanced over at Takitsubo, just barely sitting up in a small chair, and another girl of about ten years, lying asleep on a bed. She'd been called one of the oddest names Hamazura had ever heard— Last Order. Was that an ability name or something?

"I'll start with my conclusion."

Elizalina pointed to Takitsubo, then Last Order, from her bed.

"The girl in the tracksuit, I think I can manage. The little girl's condition doesn't look promising. That is all."

"…" Accelerator, still leaning against a wall, twitched an eyebrow.

Hadn't Last Order come here first?

Hamazura blinked; Elizalina had made the declaration calmly— or put another way, cruelly. "Uh, wha?" he stammered. "What do you…? You think you can manage?"

"I suppose you wouldn't understand if I told you it was *sorcery.*"

"What?"

"I suppose you wouldn't understand if I told you it was *sorcery,*" she repeated. She didn't seem willing to proceed with the conversation until he offered some kind of reaction.

Hamazura nodded for now. Sorcery? What's sorcery?

"Leaving aside whether *it* really exists or not," she said casually, cutting out the most important point, "you are familiar with how witches and whatnot have always done occult rituals since ages past, right? Leaving aside whether they have any real effect, in an era when people believed in *it*, you know that rituals were performed based on a certain sequence of actions, right?"

"What, like wrinkly old women stirring big cauldrons and stuff?"

"You understand that such rituals used all sorts of herbs—well, in modern day, plants close to what we refer to as narcotics, as well as poison taken from animals and such, right?"

"??? Hang on a second. What does all this have to do with Takitsubo's symptoms?"

The cause of Takitsubo's affliction was Crystals, created by Academy City's science and technology. All this talk of strange, occult spells didn't seem very helpful for fixing it.

"Leaving aside for now whether *it* is simply a hallucination or whether it truly provided supernatural effects," she said, sounding strangely like she was implying something, "it means that since rituals that dealt with poison were so rampant, they would have orally passed down methods to perform them safely. For example, training yourself to grow used to the poison little by little so you don't break down. Or antivenom methods that heal by removing the toxins accumulated in the body."

"That's— Uh, what do you...?" Hamazura almost shot out of his seat. "You mean you can cure her?!"

Elizalina stopped him with a hand. "That's right. The girl in the tracksuit and the little girl each have their own symptoms. The little girl essentially has toxins perpetually being injected into her, so even if you remove it temporarily, it'll fill back up again. But with the girl in the tracksuit, she should manage if we can remove what's accumulated inside her. I don't mean to say that I can completely cure her, but she'll be a lot better off than she has been."

Was Elizalina talking about the Crystals? Either way, her theory was correct—if they could remove the Crystals from Takitsubo's body, she might not see a full recovery, but her condition would immediately improve. He was suspicious of how far civilian medicinal methods could go when dealing with Crystals developed by the cutting-edge Academy City, but even health methods that seemed fake at a glance sometimes revealed scientific underpinnings if examined closely, and it wasn't rare that new medicinal techniques were devised based on such inspired breakthroughs.

"...Okay."

Slowly, hope was building inside Hamazura.

Without thinking, he embraced Takitsubo.

"Hell yeah!! We did it, Takitsubo. It's a little different from what we planned, but coming to Russia was the right move after all!"

"Hamazura. You're hurting me."

"Sorry! But I just, I just…!!"

Seeing that Hamazura was on the verge of tears, Takitsubo, even as she complained, softened her expression a little and gently rubbed his back.

"…"

Meanwhile, Academy City's strongest Level Five leaned against the wall quietly, arms folded.

This place held no clues to save Last Order, either.

Just a few hours earlier, hearing that news might have caused intense impatience and fear to burn within him. Or maybe he would have raged, demanding that Elizalina relieve Last Order's pain, even for a second or less, claiming even a futile struggle was enough for him.

Something inside him seemed to be changing, little by little.

Like how steel's properties changed after burning ardently, then suddenly cooling down.

…Yelling and throwing a temper tantrum isn't going to make the situation any better, he thought, digesting everything he had learned. *Either way, I know we don't have much time. Which means I definitely don't have time to waste on pointless shit anyway. If I struggle for stopgap measures and use up all the time I've gained, it'll catch up to us in the very end.*

Making the decision immediately, Accelerator took out the sheaf of parchment. "Feel free to give your treatment in your way. But first, answer my question. Can you read this thing?"

"Given time, I believe there's a possibility I could." Elizalina nodded slightly. "The text on the surface is only a foothold for decoding the contents. From what I can see, it looks like Russian Catholic, so I might be able to, but it will probably take a while. Do you want to leave it with me anyway?"

"No." Accelerator waved the parchment a little as if to confiscate it. "I just needed to know if it was possible. You focus on treatment."

"I..."

And then Hamazura, who had been listening to them, opened his mouth to speak.

But he couldn't form any actual words.

Accelerator sniffed at him. Maybe the guy assumed being openly joyous about his own companion being saved was rubbing salt in Accelerator's wound, since there was no end in sight for him yet.

"I don't have time, either. I'm gonna get going, if you don't mind."

As Accelerator moved toward the door on his crutch, it wasn't the speechless Hamazura but Elizalina who asked him this, not particularly hopefully: "Any leads?"

"Maybe not, but I'll find one."

After leaving the hospital room, Accelerator called out to a soldier walking down the passage. This wasn't a peacetime medical facility. Originally, it was a fortress designed for war—they'd simply lugged some medical equipment inside. It was more military than anything else.

"How are those spies I weeded out?"

"We're, uh, interrogating them, but things don't look hopeful," said the soldier, withering. "We're not experts at coaxing people to talk, and Russian spies get assigned to several small cells for a single operation. It's possible they don't even know any intel beyond what they needed."

"That so."

"Where are you headed? I can bring you there if you want."

"Don't bother," Accelerator said, waving a hand haphazardly at him. "I'll try going after an information source who's a bit more reliable."

The soldier frowned, but Accelerator wasn't duty-bound to explain anything more to him.

After leaving, Accelerator walked through the long passage to a different hospital room from Elizalina's. Without knocking, he opened the door.

The occupant was someone that, strangely, wasn't tied up.

Maybe that was another of the Level Zero's ideas.

"...Misaka Worst," he muttered.

The girl sitting on the bed, who looked about high school age, looked at him with a scornful glare.

A unique human clone created in a project called the Third Season, based on the third-ranked Level Five's somatic cells.

She wore mostly white combat gear for her clothing, but her right arm hung from a cast and a belt. Accelerator had snapped it when he became enraged during their battle. She had large pieces of gauze in other places, too, like from behind her ear to the back of her neck.

Two enemies.

Two people who would stab each other in the heart without so much as a word passing between them.

"What might'cha be lookin' for today?"

Just by shfiting a few millimeters, Misaka Worst created an expression that would have made anyone uncomfortable.

It seemed almost as though she'd prepared it beforehand.

"If you saved Misaka in that situation, her only value would be information. Unfortunately for you, Misaka doesn't have the programming to tell you whatever you want. Which means it's as clear as fire what happens next. Still, even though it was necessary, healing Misaka only to break her all over again shows what good taste you have."

"Help me."

"With what? Why? How?"

"The Russians planted some bugs and I found a bunch. They'll spit out fragments of information, some real and some lies. Figure out which is which for me. With your knowledge, I might find a clue."

"Your reasoning?"

"The timing of your attack." Accelerator shook the rolled-up stack of parchment. "It was right after I tried to ask some lady named Vodyanoy about this parchment. Your interruption felt contrived. Maybe they were just manipulating you to make sure I didn't find a lead. It's possible that if I combine the intel in your head and the Russian spy information, I'll come up with something."

"Not that. What's your reasoning that Misaka needs to help you?"

Misaka Worst grinned.

Her words seemed to purposely place herself in a dilemma. Perhaps a person who had gazed upon a world through eyes laden with malice wouldn't feel any hesitation at being hurt.

However.

His face remaining steady, Accelerator answered, "The Third Season isn't on the winning side or anything, here. Unless you're more of an idiot than I thought, you know that."

"..."

"Those guys in Academy City plan to use the Misaka network for *something*. Meanwhile, you came after the kid and me to reconnect the malfunctioning network...But why? I don't know how many thousands of somatic cell clones have been created since the Third Season got going for real, but if you're all the new network, you share the same fate. Either someone will use and discard you for their own ends, or they'll reconstruct the network without even being able to do that. Whichever happens, you're stuck. We're talking about people who consider the slaughter of twenty thousand puppets to be a *success*. I'm sure you realize they're not gonna use you in any kind of decent way."

"Is that why I have to help you?" Misaka smirked. "To join hands with not only an enemy, but one who stands at the dead center of hate and malice?"

"You said you had a mechanism that prioritizes picking up negative emotions from the network, like malice or loathing or whatever, right?"

"So what?"

"Is that shitty, evil brain of yours *really* considering something as admirable as staying loyal to your master who's using you as a disposable pawn? You know, I heard from that kid that not even one more of you can die right now."

"Even if that was true, that doesn't mean listening to you will solve anything. It would just shorten Misaka's life span, wouldn't it?"

"Yeah? Then it's time to make a deal."

"What?"

"Project Dark May."

"…You can't be serious."

"A project that tried to apply my ability-control method to boost espers' personal realities. They apparently got a little out of it, but never anything that led to a Level Five. The only way for you to be someone they can't replace is to gain abilities the other Sisters don't have. So? If you analyze my fighting style, you might be able to find a way out."

"…"

For a few seconds, there was silence.

It wasn't time used to think.

Her life wasn't important to her.

Anyone could have seen that from her words and actions thus far.

The scales of this deal tipped based on whether it would be fun. Whether it was worth getting a taste of, even if it meant turning her back on the giant organization of Academy City.

She was giving it close consideration.

Rolling the malice around in her mouth, tasting it to see if it was worthy.

And then she replied with a smile.

In accordance with her production objective, Misaka Worst took up her malice once more.

"Misaka understands…Yeah, that *would* be more like *this* Misaka. Probably more effective than bringing that painfully adorable command tower's face of suffering in, in an appeal to goodwill or charity."

"I'll find a clue to wiping out the kid's ailment. You look for a different route so they don't use you and lose you. We'll fight Academy City. We'll outsmart them. Our interests are aligned now. If you get it, quit whining and do something."

"Still, I have to say..."

Misaka Worst rose from the bed she'd been sitting on, giving a slight wave of her elbow on her right arm, fixed in place by the cast.

"They tuned Misaka specifically to kill Academy City's number one. Can't believe the day has come where even after all this, she'd give one of those insincere business smiles in agreement."

Her allusive words were probably something like a personal quirk; she expressed negative emotions from the network easily. She'd rub him the wrong way, even if she didn't mean to. Especially when it came to interactions with Accelerator, she'd always do that.

In response, Accelerator glanced at her cast, then moved his lips, his next words barely coming out.

"...Sorry. That was my bad for letting them manipulate me like that."

For a moment.

Misaka Worst's face, painted over with malice, took on an expression that really didn't seem to be thinking anything, like her thoughts had ground to a halt. Frankly speaking, it was a blank look.

"Pff-hya!"

And then.

Misaka Worst, who had just stood up on the floor on her own feet, rolled back onto the bed again.

"Ah-hya-hya-hya-hya!! What the hell?! What the hell was that about?! They went through all that to give me a body, tuned me specifically for the battlefield, and now this!! They could have at least put me at the top of the evil ladder so everyone hated me! Seeing you make such a meek little expression is really calling my own existence into question here!! Hya-hya-hya-hya-hya-hya!!"

"...To hell with villains," spat Accelerator in response as Misaka Worst held her stomach and flailed her arms and legs. "I got to the top—and that didn't make the kid's life the least bit safer. I don't have a reason to bother with that anymore."

Yes.

Neither that Level Zero nor that monster named Aiwass belonged strictly to good or evil to begin with. If he wanted to fight people like that, he couldn't stick to an easily defined side.

Tears forming in her eyes, her voice strangely refreshed in contrast to her sneering, Misaka Worst asked, "A monster like you that's so deep in the mud—even if you got out of the darkness, where would you go?"

"Hell if I know. I'll find a place," answered Accelerator, sounding for all the world like he found simply *replying* to her annoying. "Both of us are monsters those Academy City bastards purposely programmed hate into…I doubt I can abandon all that responsibility, and I don't want to think about it, but at the very least, they cast their lines, and we took the bait like dumb-ass fish. ——Which means what? Reaching the pinnacle of evil wasn't fighting against them—it was literally just running along the track we were supposed to be on."

"…"

"This time, they'll pay for this. We'll rebel against them for real. I'm sick and tired of dancing in the palm of their hand. And I don't care if it means doing things that don't suit me."

As he spoke, Accelerator slowly reached out with his free hand.

Almost as if asking for a handshake from a compatriot he'd trust his back to.

"Please."

In that instant, Misaka Worst fell silent, as though time had stopped.

But that didn't last more than a few seconds.

As if her pent-up feelings burst out all at once, Misaka Worst cradled her stomach and swung her legs around on the bed, back and forth, tears even coming to her eyes. "Hya-hya-hya-hya-hya-hya-hya-hya!! Are you stupid? Are you stuuuuuuupid or something?! Wow! That idiotically serious look is just *wow*!! Ah-hya-hya-hya-hya-hya-hya!!"

Rolling on the bed, she continued her bizarre cackle, this time

hysterical enough to make one wonder if her diaphragm had actually torn.

But eventually, she curled up, and from that position, she sprang to her feet.

She firmly grasped the hand extended to her with a *smack!!*

A sharp sound echoed in the hospital room, similar to the kind made when catching a baseball with a baseball glove.

For her as well, someone drowned in malice, the act of taking someone's hand must have demanded determination in its own right. And Misaka Worst had overcome it. Their linked hands, the handshake between two who had once been after each other's lives, proved that.

Misaka Worst stood up, hand still in the grip, like she was a wife being escorted. Giving a mean-spirited smirk, she spoke to the one who was her fated enemy. "Same goes for Misaka. But isn't this the first time you've ever held someone's hand like this?"

"…No," murmured Accelerator, looking away slightly. "I've done that a lot before—with an annoying kid who has the exact same face as you."

Recalling the one girl due to the sensation of their connected hands, he renewed his resolve.

This wasn't the end.

Once more.

Without fail.

CHAPTER 6

True Darkness Unfolding
Up_the_Castle.

1

Nothing was around.

The area was only a snowfield to begin with, but every last thing that could provide cover had been removed from around Fiamma's base. Even the ubiquitous conifer trees were absent, nevermind man-made structures. The snowfield sprawling before them was smooth, prepared in such a way to quickly locate anyone approaching and accurately fire missiles into their midst.

From a spot just outside that wall of firepower's effective range, Touma Kamijou peered down at the white snow.

And into a giant hole.

Originally, this had probably been a low hill or some similar landform. The hill's slanted surface gave way to a well-hidden tunnel about six feet across. Rather than going straight ahead, the hole appeared to lead farther downward.

"...Another secret base," he muttered, sounding half astonished. "Secret bases all over the place."

"Why are you so surprised? Japan's Academy City would be far more advanced than this. I wouldn't be surprised if a lake there split open and a giant robot came out," answered Lesser in a playful tone, going past him and slipping into the tunnel.

It wasn't pitch-black inside the tunnel, which was fully covered on all sides with snow. Naked light bulbs hung from the walls at regular intervals. As they proceeded in deeper, the space widened little by little. After walking about fifty meters, they reached a freight train stop.

But—

"...Nobody's here."

"No train, either, it seems."

At first, they'd been hiding behind objects to try to sneak a peek, but when they'd confirmed the total absence of people, they exchanged glances and stepped into the stop.

It was a different stop than the one they'd snuck into before, but the layout was similar. The differences amounted to the lack of any freight train or wooden loading containers. The space, illuminated by several light bulbs, felt unnatural, wrong—like a house the residents had left without remembering to turn off the lights.

Kamijou, drawn to the metal tracks, squatted beside them and put his ear to the cold rail. "No shaking at all. Can't smell any diesel exhaust smoke, either...It doesn't even seem like the train's running nearby."

"...Then maybe Fiamma already finished bringing the last of the supplies into his base."

"But that would mean..."

Kamijou and Lesser exchanged soured looks.

It was about twenty-five miles from here to Fiamma's base. If they couldn't sneak aboard a freight train, they'd have no choice but to go through the snowy cave on foot. It was far enough that even if they had asphalt underfoot, one big earthquake could have them designated as stranded.

Lesser put the Steel Glove on her shoulder again. "Okay—all right. I have a plan."

"R-right. I should have expected a professional sorceress to have some kind of backup plan. We can't use up all our stamina just *walking*, then face Fiamma while our calves are about to explode. It would be awful."

"Uppies, please."

"I'm going to knock your lights out."

Frustrated with himself for having embraced even a momentary hope, Kamijou looked down the long twin rails.

It looked like walking really was the only thing they could do.

Deciding it was better than going aboveground and getting pelted by the grenade launchers guarding the base, he forced himself to get pumped up.

"Let's go, Lesser. Or do you want to mind the place while I'm gone?"

"Yeah, yeah. Make sure you remember this, please. Your dear Lesser has been admirable in her unswerving loyalty."

As Lesser spoke, she moved next to Kamijou, but then for some reason positioned the Steel Glove upside down, skillfully balanced it, then straddled its grip like a witch's broomstick. The four blades wriggled and squirmed like fingers, sending her body forward.

Kamijou looked at her as though he'd discovered a traitor. "...Lesser, what's that?"

"What do you mean? I can use the Steel Glove like this, too. It does dig into me, though, in various places. I mean, Bayloupe was riding this thing all around the Tube— Hey, stop that; stop, please!! It can't hold two people, and it'll fall to pieces if your right hand touches it; please endure it and *walk by yourself*!!"

Kamijou and Lesser struggled with each other, but it didn't last long.

Not that his Imagine Breaker had broken the Steel Glove or anything.

What broke was the passage in front of them.

With an explosive *boom*, the ceiling, made of snow, abruptly collapsed.

It happened about a hundred meters ahead of them. The thick white ceiling—which was probably supported by something magical—had suddenly fallen, like a giant shutter dropping.

In the blink of an eye, the passage was blocked.

And it didn't stop there.

Right after came a bursting sound loud enough to burst eardrums.

The passage's ceiling continued to break and fall, one section at a time, as if from the foot of an approaching giant.

If it caught them, it would bury them alive.

"Crap!! Let's head to the entrance for now!!"

"You didn't need to tell me!!"

Kamijou and Lesser wheeled around and sprinted at full speed. Even as they did, the passage and rails vibrated with a low sound, the snowy ceiling about to turn into an avalanche that would swallow them whole. It was pretty much like a monster's mouth was chasing them.

"What?! Did my right hand break some spell supporting the snow?!"

"Or else it's a wonderful theme-park attraction that Fiamma thought up!! Maybe we shouldn't have tried to use the same trick…!!"

*Whump-whump…*The low noises continued.

Both Kamijou and Lesser ran as fast as they could.

As the collapse closed in on them, tiny ice particles whipped up.

The cloud quickly overtook them. The collapse was right at their heels.

But at that very moment, Kamijou's body launched out of the entrance. Next to him, Lesser, without moderating her momentum, stumbled spectacularly onto the snow. But was it really a coincidence that he could see her underwear?

Are…we good…?

Hands on his knees and breathing raggedly, Kamijou went to offer her a hand. She lay faceup on the ground, catching her breath.

But his motion stopped halfway through.

He'd figured it out.

The collapse hadn't started because his right hand had nullified sorcery holding up the snow. At the same time, it also wasn't Fiamma's side blowing up the passage to prevent their entry.

"Damn it...," he murmured, hearing a high-pitched, flutelike noise.

The true cause was...

"Academy City's bombarding the base?!"

Kamijou snatched Lesser up from the ground by the collar, swung her around, and pushed her toward the hill's slope that used to be the tunnel entrance.

A moment later, something came.

In the sky, veiled in white snow clouds, something glittered. No—it wasn't just one thing; they numbered fifty, at least. The shrill, flutelike whistling was the sound of metal tearing through the air at supersonic speed. And those hunks of metal were drop cannons—weapons that first used gunpowder to fire artillery shells fifteen centimeters across and about seventy centimeters long up into the air approximately five hundred meters, before precisely guiding them to a target by moving their tail assemblies.

There was no time to think about where they'd fall.

Besides, they weren't picking their targets carefully. They were bombarding everything, from the base itself to the sensors and other equipment deployed in the surrounding area.

Sound and light exceeding his senses' tolerance burst out, rattling Kamijou's and Lesser's bodies. The light was intense pain, and the sound was an impact. The white flash was so powerful that Kamijou couldn't tell the difference between when his eyes were closed and when they were open. Despite having Lesser pressed against the hill's slope, he could feel her slipping away from his hands. Except... that wasn't quite correct. He'd been on top of her, and now *his* body was being blown into the air by the shock waves.

Over thirty seconds of pure stupefaction.

Or perhaps it was actually only an instant, and the afterimage burned into his eyes was still overloading his senses.

"Les...ser..."

When he squeezed out a word, his voice sounded abnormally

hoarse. Pain shot past his temples, like he'd been staring at a fluorescent light for too long.

He didn't have time to leisurely tend to his wounded body.

Grrr-grrr-grrr-grrr!! Heavy-sounding caterpillar treads had reached his ears.

The smell of exhaust, the kind that would irritate your chest, mixed into the white, snowy scenery.

An Academy City mobile unit…!!

Ignoring the body heat draining from him, Kamijou buried himself deep into the snow.

He had entered Russia illegally. If they found him like this, they'd arrest him for sure. He couldn't let himself be caught now—he had to save Index.

The caterpillar-tread noise and exhaust gas came in a few different varieties.

Small, airborne tanks were at the formation's front, probably made for dropping out of transport planes and bombers, with special vehicles loaded with long-range missiles and rockets following in their wake. Many personnel carrier trucks, too, each with over twenty powered suits on board. The unarmed, armored eight-wheelers accompanying the unit could have been power supply vehicles for recharging powered suits or UAVs. The ones with all the antennas on them might have been command vehicles for controlling unmanned units deployed in the surroundings.

Sporadic artillery fire began coming from the base. The Russian military was counterattacking.

But the return fire was erratic. Academy City's first wave had probably reduced their combat strength by quite a bit. That didn't matter much if even one of those arcing projectile explosives landed nearby though, since it would turn Kamijou and Lesser into messy chunks of meat regardless of how the battle was going.

"(…Now's our chance!!)"

Then, Lesser, who had gotten close to him without him realizing, quietly spoke to him, letting herself sink into the sloped snow like he was.

Kamijou stared at her. He couldn't wrap his head around what she was saying.

"(…Our *chance*?! The Russians started shooting, too. It's gonna turn into a full-on tank battle any minute now!!)"

"(…That's why we'll use the confusion to sneak into Fiamma's base.)"

Lesser watched the powered suits closely as they got off the trucks and entered combat readiness.

"(…Why do you think the Russian military is defending? Fiamma doesn't want to move. Either he doesn't want them to know he's hiding there, or he's putting some sort of sorcery to work. Anyway, if we go now, we can get to the base from the ground. Now that the underground route is blocked off, it's our only choice.)"

Academy City and the Russian forces had begun their artillery combat.

The base, despite being dozens of kilometers away, was now within weapon range—which meant victory, essentially, was already determined. One normally positioned defensive lines farther in front than this. Either Academy City had already wiped out their defensive line, or they'd used supersonic bombers to rapidly drop forces behind it.

She was right—if they took advantage of the chaos as they charged in, they might be able to get into the facility.

"(…What do we do, then? They might be immersed in the battle, but if we just stand up and start walking, they'll see us and shoot us.)"

"(…We'll steal a powered suit.)" Lesser regripped her Steel Glove in both hands. "(…You probably don't need complicated control techniques for them. If they follow the movement of your arms and legs, even we should be able to work them without any special training.)"

"(…You make it sound so easy. Those things can withstand thirty-millimeter gatling guns. My right hand won't do anything to them. How do we take one down?)"

"(…Obviously, it's going to be *me*.)" Lesser lowered herself like a predator on the hunt, weapon in hand. "(...We don't know if they understand that base's importance, but they can't beat Fiamma with the gear they have. Fiamma doesn't seem to want to move at the moment, for some reason, but he'll show up if the base ends up at a serious disadvantage. If we can't get in before that, everyone will die.)"

"(...Lesser!!)"

"(...If you want to praise me, you can do it in bed while you pet my head.)"

Ignoring Kamijou trying to stop her, Lesser silently began to move. She seemed to be after a powered suit that had just passed nearby and now had its back to them, but the machine's hand gripped a giant shotgun. One of the anti-shelter weapons he'd spotted in Avignon, France.

Nobody could get hit by one of them and still be in any kind of shape to appear at their own funeral.

Right now, Lesser was basically trying to kill a large beast with a primitive spear or club. Maybe she had traditional techniques, too, but from what he could see from the outside, it would virtually be an acrobatic stunt.

"(...Shit!)" he murmured to himself, still deep in the snow.

He had other concerns besides Lesser.

Yes—

"(...There should be sorcerers in addition to the Russian military inside Fiamma's base. When we snuck in before, there were almost two hundred Russian Catholic sorcerers in the big room with him. If they make an appearance, they could even topple Academy City's advantage. But there's no sign of them. Does that just mean they've already joined the battle? Or have they not shown up yet? If not, then why? Even Fiamma can't possibly want that base to fall. Then why does he need to conserve them and helplessly draw Academy City's forces toward him?)"

None of these words were spoken in hope of an answer.

He was only saying them to himself so he could get a handle on what his questions were again.

And yet…

"Hmm? That's obvious. It's all to lure you in—you and your precious right hand."

…an answer came.

Dumbfounded, Kamijou searched for the source of the sound. It wasn't in front of or behind him or to the left or right. The voice had come from inside his clothes.

"I may have caused this war, but I wouldn't want your right arm to get caught up in some petty cannon fire. And if people show up saying 'We don't know what he'll use it for, but it seems essential to Fiamma of the Right's plan, so we'll just kill the kid and be done with it'—that would be an issue, too. I left a hole, I suppose you could say, on purpose, to get my hands on it quickly."

"…"

Kamijou had encountered Fiamma in the Elizalina Alliance of Independent Nations. The encounter had technically ended as a draw, but he'd stolen Sasha Kreutzev and destroyed their whole party. They'd pretty much lost that fight.

At the time, Kamijou had wondered why the man had so readily retreated. Fiamma wanted his right arm, and he'd been in full control of the battle. And yet, he'd let Kamijou escape for the sole reason that carrying both Sasha and Kamijou's right arm with him at the same time would be inefficient.

Why didn't he ever think Fiamma of the Right would come up with a plan after that? He couldn't have *only* wanted to leave them a message in bad taste.

He'd search for where Kamijou was.

And once he found him, he could attack at any time.

With accuracy and precision.

Shit…!!

Kamijou heard several shrill, flutelike noises overhead at once.

Immediately, he tried to look up.

But he was too late.

Boom!! A rumbling broke out, enough to shake the white land itself.

A rumbling from under his feet.

2

Selick G. Kirnov let out a groan.

Where am I? he wondered.

It was a dark room. His body had been tied to a chair placed in the center. In front of him, a few steps away, was an outlined square of light—probably a door, he reasoned. The light was filtering in through the gaps.

That was the only light source, however. No windows or light bulbs, so he could only see vague silhouettes of the objects near him.

Something like metal—like blood.

The smell pressed against his chest, and it gave him a bad feeling about all this.

After all.

He had an idea what was happening.

"...Let's make this quick."

He heard a voice.

And then a clack.

The sound came from in front of him. Someone had set a wooden chair down on the floor and must have sat in it. With almost no light in the room, only a pair of red eyes gazed directly at Selick.

"You can be honest. You can lie. You can even stay quiet. After all, I'll measure what's in your mind by the response you give to my questions. Think of it as an advanced lie detector. It'll all be over soon anyway."

Snap!! A pale-blue flash of light covered Selick's vision for just a moment.

He thought it was a camera.

But no. It was a spark of high-tension electrical current. It had come off of a different person, a girl standing immediately behind the red-eyed man.

"She can control electricity. That's the kind of esper she is. An esper—you know what that is, right? I know you at least get Daihasei Festival broadcasts here…and in your line of work, it's natural you'd be familiar with 'em."

"…"

Sweat broke out on Selick's face.

The red-eyed person ignored him and spoke.

"I want to know why jerks like you are hiding out around here… Oh, and again, you can answer however you want. The kid behind me is gonna measure all your brain's electrical signals anyway. Right—I know. I have an idea. Let's do it this way. I'll ask a question. What were you looking for when you came to the Elizalina Alliance of Independent Nations? And you answer like this: 'I was searching for something important on my superior's orders.' That'll be good. And then we look at your mind, see how firmly you agree or reject what you're saying, use that as a key to search the region of your brain where you store memories, and we're done. My investigative methods might lack delicacy, but eh, don't let it bother you."

Selick had received so much training not to talk.

And just as much to make them think he was confessing, when he was really passing them fake information.

However.

They'd just told him they could look into his mind whether he agreed or refused. How was he supposed to stop them from doing *that*?

In any case, Selick G. Kirnov had one thought.

Don't let them follow their plan.

If the enemy could read his mind unconditionally, they would have scooped out the necessary information while he'd been unconscious. They were only bothering to question him like this because they needed to. So if he didn't let them stick to their plan to get information, he might be able to defend it to the last.

He felt the will to resist.

He would find a thread to counterattack.

And then.

As though reacting to Selick's inner thoughts, despite him not having said a word, the red-eyed person smoothly pointed his index finger at Selick's face.

No.

Strictly speaking, *behind* him.

What's...?

Since he was tied to the chair, he couldn't see very far behind him by twisting his neck. He could only get little glimpses out of the corner of his eye.

That was when he heard the creaking.

It sounded almost like a thin rope squeezing something, but the noise was heavier and eerier.

Barbed wire.

The stench, like metal and blood, plunged through Selick's nose down into his lungs.

In the same moment, he realized what he'd gotten a glance at.

Barbed wire, hanging from fixtures in the ceiling. Its sharp barbs held about an armful's worth of flesh onto them. He didn't know what kind of flesh. It was dark red, and the skin seemed to have all been removed. But here and there, on that flesh, small bits of what looked like cloth clung to it.

Yes.

As though...

A person's head and arm had been severed, and all their skin flayed, then the remainder was tied up with barbed wire and strung up—would it turn into something like this?

"...???!!!"

Selick G. Kirnov almost lost control over his breathing. When he looked again, several other pieces of barbed wire were hanging, too. No flesh on them. Instead, seven chunks had been torn apart and were now lying on the floor. The weight had probably been too much.

Including the hanging one, there were a total of eight. Things that looked like dark-red scraps of cloth clung to them. They'd changed colors quite a bit, but he recognized them. It was the outfits they'd been wearing before.

In the dim room, the monster only noticeable by his red eyes told him quietly, "Uncooperative—every one of them. I know it's fastest to have the brat behind me read your mind, but it doesn't take much to make me violent."

Selick heard a strange *rattle-rat-rat-rat-rat-rat-rat-rat-rattle*.

It was coming from his feet. The chair's legs were tapping against the floor—in time with the strange trembling that had overtaken him.

The red-eyed person ignored it and parted his lips into a smile. Bringing his face close to Selick, he said, "We don't have any more hostages. Don't make this hard for me."

Accelerator and Misaka Worst opened the door and left the room.

The place they'd just been in wasn't a gruesome torture chamber, but a storehouse for preserving food. In fact, the Elizalina Alliance of Independent Nations apparently didn't have torture chambers to begin with.

"Well, that was pretty easy. What a bore," said Misaka Worst. "He *was* a Russian spy, right? With all that anti-torture training? I thought they all had tolerance for physical violence."

"Deception never changes. It's about not giving them a chance to make rational decisions."

He probably couldn't have gotten the spy to talk through mere violence, like punching or kicking him. Even if he'd *actually* stripped off his skin with a blade, it might not have worked.

That was why he'd needed to bluff.

Even veteran Russian spies wouldn't know how to fight against Academy City's espers. But they had probably built up a body of logic they could use to fight the unknown, the incomprehensible.

So Accelerator adopted an entirely different approach to give the man a shock.

To do that, he'd cut a bunch of beef into blocks, stuck rags to it, and wrapped it all up with barbed wire.

Confronted with that, the spy's mind, completely rattled, immediately panicked. Soldier or spy, resistance to pain wasn't because they had dull senses. It was because they trained their minds beforehand to endure it. On the other hand, if you messed up the underpinnings, you could reduce their tolerance to a child crybaby. After all, soldier or civilian, everyone was built the same way—they were all living creatures.

Accelerator rested his back against the wall.

Misaka Worst opened her mouth and spoke as if to make fun of him. "Heh. How kind of you."

"Eh?"

"Misaka has some of your behavioral patterns input into her so she can fight you. Last Order or civilians are one thing—but isn't this the first time you've settled things nonviolently against a professional enemy?"

"No point being inefficient about it. Didn't feel like messing around with human flesh anyway," he spat in response. "What? Wasn't stimulating enough for you, little lady?"

"Aw, no! Misaka loves deceiving people. ♪ Seeing a proud professional succumb to nonexistent fear and turn into a mess of tears and snot is incredible. Kya-ha! ☆"

Stretch.

Misaka Worst flashed a smile that seemed like a crushed fruit.

Accelerator tisked softly. "…What do you think of what the crybaby said?"

"Totally unnatural. I mean, the Russian military was using this war as justification to attempt a serious invasion operation—including aerial bombings—against the Alliance, since they've been after something of theirs since before, right? Strange they'd send in spies at all in that case. Normally, you have the spies withdraw before the bombing started…Unless they were disposable! Heh."

"The spies were scheduled to withdraw, but a few hours ago, they were suddenly ordered to stay. And then they even sent extra spies crawling into the Alliance."

"Hoo-whee. It's like they planned it around the Misakas coming into the country."

That was one way of looking at it.

If that was the case, the spies lurking in this military facility must have been worried to death.

They wanted to get out of the Alliance before the bombings. But their target had just set foot into a most dangerous spot on his own. To accomplish their objective, the spies, too, would have to follow Accelerator.

But.

"...Still, that spy fell for the trick too easily. Maybe it was because he couldn't fight an esper the way he envisioned it, but it didn't seem like it. It was more like he'd never considered possibly fighting against one at all and then happened to bump into one."

"Maybe it was all confidential, and they were after the Misakas, but they didn't get anything explained to them? Like they'd give the details on-site over radio or something," Misaka Worst offered with a shrug. "And what did the spy say the mission given to him was, hmm?"

"To photograph the interiors of Alliance military facilities. Their mission was sneak photography using small cameras."

"For what?"

"To bring secret documents out of the base before the real bombings began, then bring them to a specified point. The concrete instructions would have come from someone on the other side of a monitor."

As he said it, he found himself confused.

The only "document" he had was the parchment paper. Was it that essential to the Russian military's generals?

"Anyway," he said, picking himself up off the wall and leaning into his crutch again, "if we go to that specified point or whatever, we'll meet whoever needs that parchment. Who will know how to decode and use it, too."

And that might be a clue to saving the still-unconscious Last Order. In which case, he didn't have the choice not to go. Egoistic or not, he needed to have them cough up the value of a parchment they'd attack a military base for.

"Misaka loves selfish plot developments like that. It's making her hard all over. ☆"

"Shut up. The destination of the parchment delivery was a front-line Russian base near the border. I'll raid it. You do whatever you want."

"Oh, but obviously Misaka would tag along wherever there's more blood to be shed. Speaking of which, what about Last Order?"

"What would happen if I left her to you?"

"Probably something too horrible to even look at when Misaka gets bored."

As he considered punching the cackling Misaka Worst, something wavered at the edge of Accelerator's vision.

No, that wasn't it.

His vision wasn't what had wavered.

This was…

3

Deep within the military base close to the border between Russia and the Elizalina Alliance of Independent Nations, Fiamma of the Right was using a book-style Soul Arm to communicate with someone.

That someone being an authority of the Russian Church: Bishop Nikolai Tolstoj.

"Well, things are finally getting interesting," said Fiamma into the Soul Arm, lying open on the table, as he sat down in a plain chair. "To be honest—and I know I was having you cooperate with me—but your battle results here in Russia have been anything but praiseworthy. It's a pain, but this time, I'll readjust the scores."

"Say whatever you wish." Nikolai's tone was hard. *"Don't hold anything back. You told me that you'd secured Sasha Kreutzev. Use that*

weapon right now! Or have you forgotten Russian soldiers are dying as we speak?!"

"Sortie preparations are all finished. I'll bring it out soon. When I do, the battle situation will once again become opaque. Academy City's vaunted control will cease to work—and the true war will begin."

"Either way, I'm fine as long as I can achieve my objective. If our cooperation is a shortcut to that, then I will keep providing support."

"The Patriarch? You want to be the one that much? The Roman pope I know never looked as amused as you do."

"Pah—don't compare the Roman pope to our Russian one."

"Are they that different?"

"In any case," said Nikolai Tolstoj, lowering his tone and asking slowly, *"where are you right now?"*

"What would you do if you knew?"

"It can't be at the base. We lost your signal from there already."

"Ha-ha," chuckled Fiamma, who certainly should have been deep inside the "base" before answering, "you'll know soon enough... whether you like it or not."

It was easy, perhaps, to witness the phenomenon that occurred then. Few people, however, could have known what it actually meant.

The first one to notice it was likely a man from a Florence civic group.

He'd come before an old church with other companions for the preservation of historical relics. It was wartime, but the worst fires of conflict had yet to take hold in Italy. What had taken hold of the city, however, was a tense, high-strung atmosphere. Nobody knew what would cause a huge riot to break out.

He felt something like tremors from time to time. Rumors were that it was city gas lines and such being ignited while people took advantage of the chaos to set fire to buildings in acts of robbery. That was what this middle-aged man figured.

However, the one he'd just felt was different from anything thus far.

It wasn't something coming from a short distance away from the city, from the *outside*.

It had come from the *inside*.

In other words—it had echoed from inside the church.

"...?"

The middle-aged man slowly turned around.

He had a bad feeling about this.

He heard a creaking noise—emanating from that which he was trying to protect.

The historic steeple, which one could call the cornerstone of the majestic church, had broken in the middle. The structure proceeded to ignore gravity and floated up, still containing the giant bell that always announced time in the city.

Why had it broken?

Why was it floating?

He could feel the common sense within him shattering.

And...

...at that same moment, a giant steeple tore away from the Mont-Saint-Michel abbey in France.

Several pillars ripped out of St. Mary's Church in Italy.

And the grand pipe organ flew out of St. Joseph's Cathedral in India.

With over two billion followers, the Roman Church had built many churches and abbeys all over the world throughout its long history. Their forms and design philosophies varied based on the land, era, and culture, producing unique characteristics in each building.

Objects seen as particularly important had just been removed from those churches and abbeys.

They all flew toward a single point, as though drawn by a magnet. Toward Russia.

Toward the freezing-cold base where Fiamma of the Right waited.

Once the thousands, tens of thousands, hundreds of thousands of collected cultural objects had gathered in a single place, they wove together in an intricate pattern. Not like a jigsaw puzzle, designed that way from the start; no, this process was more like forcing dissimilar parts together to bring forth a new machine.

The enormous mountain of structures extended beyond the ten-kilometer-square base.

They swelled farther than that.

And the changes didn't stop there, either.

They went farther...

Boom!! The rumbling broke out from directly underneath Kamijou.

By the time he'd noticed it, he'd been thrown into the air.

Or at least, he felt like he had been.

But he hadn't really. The snowy ground he'd just been standing on had risen up, breaking free a massive part of the foundation. Buried underneath the ground was the subway line Academy City's drop cannons had obliterated. Maybe it had moved somehow in line with the changes to Fiamma's base.

Float.

For just an instant, Kamijou couldn't feel gravity.

A moment later.

The place he was standing on sheared off like a cliff. Lesser, about to launch an ambush on the powered suit nearby, turned around and stared, dumbfounded. It looked like she tried to reach out, but she was way too far away. She'd been left at the bottom of the "cliff."

"What...the...?!"

The incredible rumbling eventually forced Kamijou off his feet.

He could see Academy City tanks and powered suits, lifted up in the same manner as him, falling off the cliff's edge in disparate groups.

It was flying.

The ground Kamijou stood on—and the foundation under the base where Fiamma probably was, was flying.

While dropping the Russian military base's facilities and weapons away, along with the snow.

It immediately floated up about ten meters, then tore free of the last line of resistance. *Whump!* Accelerating, faster and faster, and all around Kamijou became fog. The abnormal, crushing pressure pushed his body to the ground. But there was no time for confusion. As he blinked, baffled, the fog that had so suddenly appeared was already gone.

Blue sky.

A hue at odds with the weather he'd seen from the surface.

The scene of white winter sky was nowhere to be found.

Kamijou knew what that meant.

We're...above the clouds?!

Bam!! went an explosion.

A supersonic bomber, no more than a pinprick in the sky moments ago, looked a lot bigger now. They'd probably taken hasty evasive maneuvers, surprised at the sudden event.

That wasn't the only sound.

Gshh-gshh-gch-gch!! A low roaring reverberated, like stone cogs turning together. The place Kamijou now stood was like a big bridge made of assembled stone. On the other side, miles and miles away, he could see a giant mass. He could see it clearly, partly because they were in midair, and no horizons or buildings were in the way of his vision, but also because the structure itself was ludicrously gigantic.

The castle-like main section stood in the center, and four extremely long bridges stretched from it in each direction. Their lengths weren't standard; one was over twice as long. If you considered the direction the fortress was traveling in as the front, and where Kamijou was as the back, the one abnormally long bridge would have been the right side. Church walls and doors and steeples from different cultures and different eras had been scraped together, and even now they were changing shapes in an intricate fashion.

Other than those structures with the weight of centuries in them were collected metal girders, pipes, and lighting equipment—more modern objects. They'd probably been installed in surface bases. All in all, they'd been brought together in a strange fusion reminiscent of a construction site at an old church.

Were they growing, or were they cannibalizing one another?

Unable to even grasp the meaning of what he was seeing, he heard a voice come to him from somewhere.

Maybe speakers or something were set up all over this flying castle. Unlike the wheat flour doll used previously, the sound came with noise.

"What I was setting up was not a giant facility or Soul Arm."

Fiamma of the Right.

Perhaps satisfied he'd confined his target, the Imagine Breaker, to the firmament, his voice sounded somehow amused.

"It was a place to assemble this. I had things saved up for it all over the world. I only needed to dig into my own savings. Still, to create it, I had to prepare an area for the work, like a sterilized room. That was why I needed the consecration, vast funds and time, and people."

Even now, the strange fortress Kamijou was looking at was expanding. It was essentially an explosion of stone.

"Material quantity wasn't the issue. The important thing was to create a cycle for it to expand itself. Once that cycle is complete, it can swell as large as I need it to without supplying it."

Wham!! The stony blast wind shot past Kamijou.

Though he'd just been standing on a stone bridge a moment ago, now he was suddenly inside an old-fashioned room. There were dozens of miles between here and Fiamma's base. Did that mean his fortress had already stretched out this far?

"…You sure putting me on this thing wasn't a mistake?"

"Quite the opposite. Your right arm is absolutely essential for my objective." Fiamma even laughed a little, meaningfully, before saying, *"I welcome you—to my fortress, the Star of Bethlehem."*

The Star of Bethlehem.

Fiamma of the Right had said its name, which meant even that would contain deep religious and magical meaning.

From the way he spoke, it actually seemed like it was acutely related to the entire string of events—his manipulation of the Roman Church, his kidnapping of Index and Sasha, his triggering of World War III, and his attempt to steal Kamijou's right arm:

This fortress, over three thousand meters in the air, now sat above the clouds.

Its sides reached out dozens of kilometers from the center.

It was an exceedingly impossible sight, possibly even as big as a floating Academy City would be.

Of course…

If you had the necessary mechanisms to give buoyant force to the mass and weight before his eyes, objects would float no matter how big they expanded. It was the same as a balloon—didn't matter if it was small or big. That was how science worked. In that sense, making a huge fuss about a giant object floating might have been nonsense.

But the problem lay not in the logic or theory. The pure stability with which this man-made structure floated through the air— Had something like that ever existed in the history of humanity?

It was the meaning of the word *unprecedented*.

When boats were created. When cars were created. When airplanes were created.

This was one of those times.

An opportunity had been created—one so exceedingly powerful it could decisively distort the territory that *humanity* could control.

That feeling of abnormality wrapped over his whole body, whether he liked it or not.

Sure, it may have been a grand achievement, but at the same time, a great unease came over him—the fear that perhaps it had a darker side to rival it.

"…"

But Kamijou's spirit wouldn't break there.

He wouldn't let it bother him.

The only thing he needed to do was take down Fiamma and destroy the Soul Arm remotely controlling Index.

He was almost frightened at being locked in this insanely huge fortress, but once he calmed down, he realized he had more hope here than in being left on the ground.

Giving a short exhalation, Kamijou eventually stood up.

He was worried he'd get altitude sickness after suddenly being launched up into the air, but other than a mild pain shooting through his temples, he didn't have any serious nausea, breathing issues, or narrowed vision. No problems that would prevent him from acting.

...The air pressure and temperature are the same as on the surface...? Is there some kind of weird field around this?

Come to think of it, he thought he remembered the snow splitting apart in an unnatural way the moment the fortress had broken through the clouds. Maybe it was protected by a force field in the shape of a sphere squeezed in on the top and bottom or something.

He couldn't really calculate how much effort it would have taken to do that magically.

But just like how a fortress this big was floating in the sky, it had to require immense resources and labor...Like the combined power of an organization encompassing two million followers.

Enough so that one could call it a symbol of that.

...He went through all the trouble to make this stupidly big facility. I don't know what he's ultimately after, but he probably needs the Star of Bethlehem for it, he thought, glancing at his right hand.

When he pressed his palm to a random wall, orange light ran through it like cracks, and about three feet of the wall surrounding that spot broke. However, by some sort of power, the fragments didn't fall, instead floating in the air and apparently trying to get back to their original positions. There was probably a core.

...In that case, if I destroy the core, I can deal a lot of damage to Fiamma, too. While I'm looking for him, I'll do everything I can, wherever I can. The enemy could use it in the war, after all. Don't need to leave it alone.

A *boom* hit Kamijou's ears.

Windows were fitted in the stone room, but their glass shattered. Kamijou, who had reflexively covered his ears, looked outside and saw several fighter jets dancing in the blue skies.

Academy City fighters.

Crystallizations of the latest strides in science, crisscrossing through the Russian sky.

Fiamma must have seen them, too—he made this declaration in a slightly more impassive voice.

He sounded like someone had thrown a wet blanket over his fun.

"The angelic medium, Sasha Kreutzev. The 103,000 grimoires' remote-control Soul Arm. The ritual site, the Star of Bethlehem. And your right hand, suitable to wield my power. I've acquired everything I need, so I will have to ask the supporting actors to leave."

Kamijou had a bad feeling about this.

But if he couldn't figure out where Fiamma was in this huge fortress, he didn't have any way of stopping his words.

And then.

Fiamma of the Right quietly offered:

"Sally forth, Archangel Gabriel, the POWER OF GOD. *Blow them all to bits."*

Boom!!!!!!

The world shifted to night.

In the span of a moment, the sky changed to one completely painted in black.

"That...can't be...," murmured Kamijou in a daze, confronted with powerful sorcery that held even the location of the earth, the moon, and the sun in its hands.

It wasn't that he couldn't comprehend the phenomenon before him.

He knew what it was—and that knowledge made his eyes widen to their limits as he began to tremble.

He'd witnessed it before.

An angelic spell.

A supernatural phenomenon that ultimately became the bridge toward an even greater spell of purging, one that interfered with the very movement of celestial bodies and strengthened the user's power to the point where it was possible to obliterate all humankind without even twitching a fingertip. In which case, it was obvious what one should call a being who could use it.

Kamijou's face lost more color than the night sky had as Fiamma's words continued unchallenged and amused, like a soldier during a training drill, showing off a weapon he was proud of.

"Actually, maybe in this case, I should call it Misha Kreutzev."

A moment later, Kamijou got a glimpse of some sort of blue point of light in the jet-black night sky.

If he strained to see it, it may have resembled a human figure. That was how tiny this light was, that appeared as a mere speck, and how far away it was.

However.

Sound ceased.

Something like giant wings extended from the blue speck of light, cutting horizontally through the heavens, as far as the eye could see.

The sound of an explosion ripped past Kamijou's ears moments later.

The unmanned fighter squadron storming about high over Russia exploded, wiping out the dozen or so jets all at once. Several of the ones that had moved more organically—probably manned— had their main wings severed, and Kamijou could see from the parachutes that the crews were frantically ejecting.

The destruction didn't stop there.

That blue dot of light must have only flapped its gigantic wings to blow away the unmanned fighter squadron coming its way. But those giant wings destroyed themselves partway through, everything from halfway down breaking off and flying. A huge explosion went off near the horizon where they'd landed.

Enormous clouds of earthen fragments danced into the air.

An entire mountain was completely destroyed.

"Well, I suppose the foundation itself, Angel Fall, was nothing more than a coincidental spell. A summoning method based on a further derivation of it must have some issues with stability."

This was insane.

The numbers difference had been reversed in an instant.

This was what angels were.

Beings that simply reigned with absolute supremacy.

"Still, now things are getting interesting, aren't they? The science side has been unveiling all kinds of secret weapons—it's only right that the sorcery side should eventually respond in kind."

And deep within the fortress, Fiamma smiled.

…The Star of Bethlehem is still incomplete. I lifted it up in order to panic Academy City's surface units, but now that I've had Misha Kreutzev act, my victory is assured.

Yes.

Something was missing.

"That parchment."

The Soul Arm Fiamma had acquired was for freely accessing Index, who possessed 103,000 grimoires. But that alone wasn't enough. Several pieces of knowledge were missing regarding truly esoteric secrets, such as angels and God's Right Seat. The parchment was to complement that. Once he obtained that bridge of knowledge and fed it back into the Star of Bethlehem, only then would Fiamma of the Right's plans come to fruition.

"Now, then," he said in a leisurely tone. "Time to go retrieve it, Misha Kreutzev. He may be weak, but that's no reason to show mercy. Don't hesitate, now—use all your power to bring it to me."

INTERLUDE FOUR

Mikoto Misaka witnessed the change as well.

She was on board an Academy City HsB-02 supersonic bomber. Of course, it wasn't because she was participating in regular military operations of any kind. What she was doing was mostly…no, it was *entirely* a hijacking. She'd stuck the underworld special forces team that was supposed to be on this plane in a District 23 hangar.

Despite its mammoth length of over eighty meters, the only window it had was the one in the front of the cockpit, perhaps because it was a bomber jet. Mikoto had been in the cockpit out of coincidence. Not only windows—the only actual seating in the whole craft was located here.

She showed her cell phone screen to the pilot, saying, "Anyway, get close to here. I'll jump out with a parachute after that, and then I'll be out of your hair. Once you finish your job, you can do whatever you want."

On the screen was a still image from a recorded news broadcast.

It was a reporter trying to report on something with a snowfield as a backdrop, but in the corner of the screen, it showed an Asian boy who appeared to be a civilian.

It was a poor excuse for a telop, and it even displayed the city from which it was relayed. *Go there* was the order from this pretty little tyrant.

"...D-do you have any idea how risky it is to do something like this?"

"Something like this?" Mikoto frowned. "So you don't think anything of yourselves for trying to do *something like this*? They were originally sending a professional team of assassins against a single high school student, right? That doesn't make you feel anything?"

"..."

"It doesn't matter how much risk is involved or whatever. One of us is putting all his energy into killing a run-of-the-mill high school kid, and one of us is putting all *her* energy into saving a run-of-the-mill high school kid. Which would you want to stick with? Which would you be prouder of?" she asked dispassionately.

The pilot quieted down.

Mikoto didn't think of herself as a particularly good person, nor did she assume everyone she saw, without exception, was a walking lump of kindness. After the incident involving the Sisters and Accelerator, she knew just how dark the shadows lurking in Academy City were—and just how ruthless these creatures called *humans* could be.

However.

She thought this, too, at the same time:

Not every single person in this world was, without exception, a terribly dark person. Just like that boy had reached out with his right hand and saved her and the Sisters from that hellish experiment, just like the Sisters who had risen again to answer her call, most people had, along with hopeless darkness and greed, a slight but reassuring light residing within them.

In fact, that was probably why the pilot had gone quiet.

That was why he hadn't been able to laugh it off, even though he was fully steeped in the shadows of an underworld organization.

...Sheesh. This really isn't my MO. Did something weird infect me? Mikoto scratched her head. *All of this is that idiot's fault! For now, as*

soon as I see him, I'm punching him in the face!! That's all— Strategy meeting over!!

And then it happened.

It was sudden.

Grwohhh!! Something gigantic had rapidly risen from out of the white clouds below. This supersonic bomber was quite big in its own right, over eighty meters long, but this object was so huge it made the bomber look like a tiny winged insect in comparison. A giant structure, dozens of miles long. It was like an entire city had floated up into the air—a sight that ignored scientific sensibilities (even for Academy City, commonly ridiculed as residing outside the realm of common sense).

It sported a ridiculous design.

The foundation was a big lump of *stuff*, torn from stone buildings of varying times and cultures, then kneaded together like a ball of clay. Plus, even now, like a cogwheel or a creature, it was changing shape from moment to moment.

...What the heck is that?

Mikoto moved closer to the reinforced glass, her eyes glued to the mass.

Wouldn't a structure that big floating in the air be a new world record? She didn't see any wings, rocket engines, or anything like them—in which case, how had it ensured buoyancy? Was the inside hollow, like a balloon or an airship?

Also...

...why's it wriggling like that? Or is it better to treat it more like a big cluster of independently operating robots?

But what Mikoto was really surprised about wasn't the giant mass itself.

On its edge.

On the end of a structure that stretched out like a bridge, she saw a familiar spiky-haired boy...or so she thought.

No...way...?!

By the time Mikoto did a frantic double-take, the supersonic bomber had already passed by. The window only went so far, so even if she turned her head, she couldn't see any more.

She was dumbfounded at the unexpected sight, but the pilot couldn't stay that calm.

The supersonic bomber's fuselage was about to collide with a steeple sticking straight out sideways from the mass.

He hurriedly pulled the yoke, and with a *whump*, inertial forces went to work. For Mikoto, who wasn't wearing a seat belt, it resulted in a pseudo zero-gravity experience. Albeit only for a few seconds, her body floated into the air.

Then she dropped back into her seat with a slam. But she didn't have time to complain.

This time, the blue sky, ignoring all weather patterns because they were above the clouds, suddenly changed to midnight, like someone had flicked off a light switch. Combined with the giant structure, dozens of miles long, she could only assume the sight was some kind of prank.

In the darkness bloomed a light.

A moonlike glow, pressing up against the inky sky.

But no.

What it really was…was a humanoid silhouette, floating idly in the sky, ignoring gravity. It was too far away for her to make out its expression. But she could say this for sure: That was no normal human.

After all, something that looked like wings had sprouted from its back.

Strange, inexplicable wings, like crystals, or perhaps a peacock's plumage. The shortest were under a meter long—the longest were over a hundred. Dozens of the wings had sprouted, all differing in length.

Mikoto had no time to wonder about it.

The wings flapped.

Despite their gigantic size, mere hundred-meter appendages wouldn't reach them—the sky was too large a place for that. The supersonic bomber had indeed already flown far, far away.

And yet.

With a *snaaaap!!*
The HsB-02's fuselage, made of the latest nonmetal materials, suddenly tore in half.

A slash had ripped the cockpit lengthwise. No, that was wrong. One attack, a single hit, had thoroughly sliced through a giant almost eighty meters long.

"Are you *kidding* me?!"

Mikoto felt on her cheeks the piercing chill that came at high altitudes.

A moment later, her body was launched out of the plane and into the sky, three thousand meters in the air.

She couldn't even cry out.

Out of the corner of her eye, she saw the pilot who had been with her going into a spinning fall, parachute still on his back. He looked like he could be helpful, but she couldn't depend on him right now. He didn't have any responsibility to save her, after all.

But stronger than Mikoto's fear of falling was her anger at the giant structure currently getting farther away. Even now, her body was headed straight through the clouds and toward the ground. She'd finally gotten her hands on something—and now she could clearly feel it slipping through her fingers.

Still, it wouldn't do any good to die like this.

Ugh!! What...? What do I do?!

Switching her train of thought, she directed her gaze toward the ground. There wasn't even a thousand meters left until impact.

And then, far below, she spotted a hunk of metal.

An attack helicopter.

She couldn't tell whether it belonged to Academy City or the Russian military, but she'd gladly use anything she could.

She used magnetism.

Not to attach herself to the chopper—given her altitude and speed, any unequipped body would simply get smashed upon contact. The important thing here was not too much magnetism, so she wouldn't fully attach to her target.

Her body hurtled right past the attack helicopter.

The force didn't entirely plaster her to the aircraft, but it did still push her toward it. It slowed Mikoto's speed of descent softly like a cushion. Strengthening the magnetic force in stages, finely adjusting it so the impact of deceleration wouldn't crush her, she managed to avoid a lethal falling velocity and continued without hesitation toward the white snowfield.

The helicopter jerked and slowed as well.

From the side, it might have looked like she was descending from the helicopter via an invisible rope.

Once she had her feet on the snow, she cut off the magnetic force completely.

"Anyway..."

She was in the middle of a battlefield. The wilderness had very few man-made objects on it, and Academy City and Russian tanks and armored vehicles had deployed sparsely into the area. Perhaps naturally, the wrecks were all originally on the Russian side.

Getting a whiff of the unpleasant odor of burning fuel, Mikoto looked up into the sky.

Even using her powerful manipulation of magnetic forces, she probably couldn't jump three thousand meters into the air from here.

"How am I gonna get above the clouds?" she muttered before hearing the crunch of feet on snow.

She checked the magnetic fields and sensed a person about ten meters behind her.

She turned around sharply—

"...You..."

—only to stop.

The person's expression remained the same.

Holding not an Academy City F200R but a rifle made of wood and metal called a Kalashnikov, the girl said, "Misaka's serial number is 10777, explains Misaka politely to the dumbfounded Original."

"You mean to tell me you're working with an Academy City affiliate in Russia?!"

"The withdrawal battle has ended, so I decided to spend the rest of my time on personal affairs, reports Misaka on her holiday spirit while holding a dangerous rifle in one hand."

"Personal affairs…," repeated Misaka, appalled.

Misaka number 10777 pointed overhead. "Is the Original not here on personal affairs herself? asks Misaka for confirmation."

"…Well, it's not for business…"

CHAPTER 7

Angel of Slaughter in the Skies
MISHA_the_Angel_"GABRIEL."

1

The colossal tremors also struck the field hospital in the Elizalina Alliance of Independent Nations.

At the time, from a short distance away, Shiage Hamazura was watching the "healing" Elizalina was performing on Rikou Takitsubo.

Takitsubo was lying on a makeshift stretcher, hooked up to a clear oxygen mask. Rather than an oxygen tank, the other end of the tube was connected to something that looked like several dried plants ground into incense. They would apparently remove the Crystals that had accumulated in Takitsubo's body, according to Elizalina, but...

That was when the massive shaking occurred, and Takitsubo's body fell from the stretcher onto the floor.

"Oh, shit! What is this?! Takitsubo!!" cried Hamazura before trying to run over to her, but Elizalina stopped him with a hand.

With morbidly slender fingers, she removed Takitsubo's mask and said, "She's fine. And the treatment is finished, too. The toxins have been removed from her body."

"..."

She said it so easily it didn't feel real to Hamazura.

The Crystals problem standing in their way had been so massive. And now...?

It was, so simply, *gone*?

Elizalina's additional explanation helped to ease his unnerved state: "Still, this only removed the unassimilated toxins. It didn't cure entire already-affected sections. You'll need to search for a different approach to cure the drug's lingering aftereffects," she said, putting out the tiny kindling smoldering in the incense. "...Raising one's abilities through forceful methods will only worsen the feedback. I have never exactly appreciated this so-called scientific efficiency."

Then the door flew open with a *bang!!*

Accelerator appeared.

"You— Did you see outside?! The hell's going on, damn it?!"

"It must be Fiamma. To think he would shake the four planes..."

Elizalina frowned, then disappeared out the doorway Accelerator was standing in. Though the building they were in was a field hospital, it was originally an old fortress. It didn't have any windows, so they couldn't tell what it was like outside.

Hamazura was curious, too, but right now, Takitsubo mattered more.

She'd fallen on the floor, so he went to pick her up to return her to the stretcher. But then he noticed something strange. When he lifted her, she didn't feel like a bag packed with mud like she had before. She was lighter. She was actually paying attention, attempting to shift her body weight.

Her consciousness had returned, properly reaching all her extremities.

More than anything else, that was a massive sign of improvement for Hamazura.

"Hamazura...?"

"You'll be okay," he reassured her, before losing all his energy in relief.

He had somehow ended up being held in Takitsubo's small hands instead of the other way around, so Hamazura decided he would at least keep his mouth working. "I'll explain everything to you later. Just let me say this now—you're going to be okay. You're not fully cured, and we'll probably need Academy City to completely deal with the aftereffect stuff. But for now, the Crystals won't make your condition any worse than this. Our lives aren't even in danger anymore. So you'll be okay...And now it's our turn to go on the attack."

He felt Takitsubo's body's warmth for the first time—the physical warmth any normal girl would have.

She didn't feel unnaturally warm, like she would if she was running a fever.

After briefly checking her over, he eventually left Takitsubo's embrace, little by little.

She could stand on her own two feet now.

As she sat down on the stretcher, Hamazura spoke to her again in slow tones. "I'll go call a nurse. Do you need water? If you're hungry, I can have them get some fruit, too."

"Hamazura. What do we do now?"

"If we're serious about going toe to toe with Academy City, we can't stay here forever. We threw off their pursuit by going to groud in the Alliance, just like we planned. Next is going back into Russia and searching for a way to negotiate with them."

After saying all that, he paused.

Looking into Takitsubo's eyes, he said, "But I'm not saying we have to do it together. You're still recovering. You can wait here—"

"Hamazura," interrupted Takitsubo, "which would wake you up: a kiss or a slap?"

"When you put it like that, it only makes me want to leave you here more." Hamazura roughly ran a hand through her hair and looked toward the door. "I'll find us some transportation. I'd feel bad stealing a car from the folks who saved us, but—"

Then.

It happened.

Out of the corner of his eye, he saw scattered documents. This was a temporary field hospital, but originally it was an Alliance military facility that had been furnished with medical equipment.

Because the Alliance had hastily converted it into a medical facility, military-related devices and documents would probably still be around.

The documents that had caught his attention turned out to be a bundle of faxes.

Hamazura couldn't read Russian, but he recognized the attached photograph.

It was the settlement where Digurv and the others were from.

"...Regarding the Alliance of Independent Nations' admission applicants and their problems."

Takitsubo, peering at it from behind Hamazura, read the Russian written on the report to him. Hamazura frowned and said, "You mean...Digurv's settlement wanted to be part of the Alliance?"

To begin with, the settlement was near the border with the Elizalina Alliance of Independent Nations—and an area that was being requisitioned by the Russian military. They'd scattered land mines almost as harassment, and there was also the privateer raid to think about. The desire to join the Alliance as a member to escape Russian oppression wasn't that strange.

But as anyone could tell from its current state, the people of this country hadn't accepted Digurv's settlement into the fold, and they were suffering right outside the border.

What did the report mean when it said *problems*?

"It doesn't look like it's a problem with the settlement or the people living there."

"What does that mean?"

"It says there's a Cold War nuclear missile silo near the settlement. Because of its load out, it was separated from normal military bases and hidden in the forest."

Hamazura was dumbstruck at Takitsubo's words.

She flipped through the report. "The silo itself has been left there for decades. The actual missiles have been removed, too. It's nothing but ruins now. But if the Alliance tried to annex the settlement and the surrounding land, they're worried others would assume they were trying to acquire Russian nuclear launch facility know-how. It says they can't aid the settlement, no matter how much they ask."

"That's bullshit...," spat Hamazura softly.

That nuclear launch silo didn't belong to Digurv and the others. Russia made the facility without asking them—that was why the settlers had lost their freedom, and why they were currently under the threat of land mines and privateers. It was good that an Academy City presence had arrived, but if they'd come any later, all the settlers might have been killed.

"The Kremlin Report...?"

But the injustice didn't stop there.

Takitsubo picked up another report and said, "...Hamazura, this is bad."

"What is it? A report? That diagram looks like the area's climate data."

"These numbers are measurements for wind direction, temperature, and humidity. I think the data's for predicting how bacteria will proliferate, but..."

"...Bacteria?"

Hamazura's shoulders stiffened at the ominous word.

Still looking at the stack of faxes—the Kremlin Report—Takitsubo said, "This was sent by the Russian military. They faxed the original Kremlin Report and additional documents here all at once. It seems like they want to make a show of giving Alliance officials a warning in order to justify the regular military actions happening inside their borders. This was actually only sent a few hours ago, and even if they showed the Alliance this, they'd never be able to start a large-scale evacuation. I think this is a threat against the Alliance. They're saying *You're next.*"

"What do you mean *bacteria*? How is that connected to Digurv and the others?!"

"It looks like a procedure for protecting nuclear launch facilities called the Kremlin Report was officially announced by the Russian military. The plan involves deploying bacteriological weapons to retake captured launch facilities or to protect sites on the verge of being captured. They're…"

"They're going to use the nuclear launch silo near their settlement?! It's their own country! Do the people in the Russian army plan on deploying the bacteria indiscriminately?!"

Hamazura felt dizzy.

But considering the relative locations of the nuclear launch silo and the Academy City force stationed at Digurv's settlement to protect it, he couldn't deny the possibility that they'd be a target for this so-called Kremlin Report procedure.

"Doesn't it say nobody's used the silo for decades? And they removed all the missiles, too, right?"

"The site's launch function itself still works. And they can bring in missiles from outside. Russia has only recently managed to deploy prototype missile-defense networks. They have them concentrated on the borders—they didn't consider setting up defenses for anything firing at them from a silo within the country's interior."

"…You mean that if you fired a missile from that silo, you could get it to land anywhere you wanted?"

"The Russian generals were the ones who developed this—they would know the fear of ballistic missiles flying overhead better than anyone. I think they'd do anything to stop that from happening."

"Damn it…"

At this rate, the Russians would chalk it up as something necessary to defend Russian soil and deploy deadly pathogens in the vicinity of the nuclear launch silo. If that happened, Digurv's settlement would get caught up in it, too. The germ was clearly bad enough to be labeled a *weapon*. He didn't even want to think of the death rate it was capable of achieving.

"When do they plan on deploying it?"

"I can't tell. It seems like there's not much chance the bacteriological weapon will reach the Alliance because of the overriding wind direction, but if it really gets dangerous, I think that Elizalina person will issue an evacuation advisory to the people."

Hamazura and Takitsubo didn't know when the weapon would be used.

For all they knew, the Russian military might have been carrying out the operation even as they spoke. Hamazura couldn't deny the possibility that if he and Takitsubo attempted to stop it, they might arrive just in time to get caught in the attack, too.

However.

"Takitsubo. Will you wait here for me?"

"Are we going to use the bacteria-wall military technology in the Kremlin report as a bargaining chip to negotiate with Academy City? Military-grade bioweapons by itself won't be special for Academy City—"

"Not that," denied Hamazura shortly. "I can't leave Digurv and the others there. I know all we'd be doing is taking a huge risk, but I don't want to abandon them. This is all wrong, isn't it?! It's not like I've lived a decent life before this; I've hurt a lot of people, but this is so much worse than that. Wanting to stop this from happening isn't crazy. The fact that it could happen in the first place is what's really crazy!! How is everyone doing all this shit with a straight face?!"

"..."

Rikou Takitsubo stared into Hamazura's eyes for a moment.

Eventually, she nodded, too.

"Okay. I'm going with you."

"Takitsubo?"

"I couldn't talk much while we were in the settlement, but I remember everything those people did for me. I want to fight for their sake, too."

"I hope you don't regret this."

"You too."

They exchanged nods, then headed for the hospital exit together.

He knew it wasn't the time to be doing something like this. They hadn't found any leverage they could use to negotiate with Academy City yet, and simply getting involved in the now full-fledged war playing out in Russia, a battle that had nothing to do with them, might cost them their lives. Taking an unnecessary detour amid all that would only shorten their life spans.

Shiage Hamazura went over all those factors in his mind.

Then, a single thought came out on top:

But we owe them.

2

He heard a cry.

It wasn't human.

This roar was more alien, slipping effortlessly into human minds, shaking their emotions without choice. He wanted to reject it even more than the sound of nails on a blackboard, and yet, the very thought of rejecting it summoned an incredible sense of guilt—an incomprehensible, unacceptable, unignorable cry. Breaking the limits of human hearing, the voice reverberated across the night battlefield that looked like it had a coat of India ink.

An angel.

Gabriel—the POWER OF GOD.

Misha Kreutzev.

"St…stop…"

Kamijou's mouth moved on its own.

Something stood out on the expansive battlefield like a lone light in a field of shadow. It was a pale-blue glow. Its silhouette, too, unnaturally still at an altitude of over three thousand meters, was almost humanlike.

Wings had sprouted from the silhouette's back.

Wings of ice, like crystals.

Their lengths were uneven. Some were only a few dozen centimeters, while others were over a hundred meters. The irregular wings each moved independently of the others, cracking into one another, flinging eerie sparks into the night. Kamijou knew that all of those wings packed enough destructive force to cleave mountains in half with a simple touch.

They undulated in a tight pack, just a tiny bit of power gathered inside them.

That, by itself, was enough.

"Nooooooooooooooooooooooooooooooooooooooooooooooooooooo ooooooooooooooooooooooooooooooooooooooooooooooooooooooooo ooooooooooooooooooooooooooooooooooooooooooooooooo!!!!!!"

Kamijou's human voice meant nothing when pitched against the flapping of such a massive set of wings.

A storm of destruction and slashing broke out. Academy City's fighters and supersonic bombers, designed with the most cutting-edge technology available, were cut into round slices. Several of the icy wings deliberately broke apart, transforming into hundreds, thousands of fragmented blades, raining down over the armored units deployed on the surface. An immense shock wave burst forth, and faint shudders even made it up to the Star of Bethlehem, still flying through the skies.

Kamijou peered down through a shattered window, but the dense cloud cover prevented him from seeing anything. There were gaps here and there, but that wasn't enough for him to confirm the fate of those below. Enormous clouds of snow had whipped up from the ground as well, forming a dense curtain.

"Damn it…"

Only one spot directly under the archangel visible in the distance, dozens of meters in radius, had opened up in the thick clouds. When it had shot all those shards down toward the ground, it had probably blown the clouds all over, creating localized weather disturbances.

Pilots he didn't know ejected from their sliced-up fighter jets, parachutes deploying moments later.

The archangel ignored them. It didn't aim its wings of ice at them, either.

But that was not out of benevolence or compassion. Gabriel flapped its ice wings at a different bomber, and the mere gusts its steely towerlike wings produced rattled the parachutes enough to cause them to fail.

The crews that bailed out might have been okay if they had spare parachutes, but otherwise, they were on a one-way road to death.

The word *war* wasn't enough to encompass this.

Divine punishment.

Kamijou gulped as the words seared themselves into his mind.

…It's not just the Star of Bethlehem. Fiamma, that bastard—did he kidnap Sasha so he could use that crazy archangel as a weapon?!

"Shit!!"

This wasn't the time to be dumbfounded. Kamijou burst out of the stone room for now, deciding to run across the Star of Bethlehem. The angel seemed to be under Fiamma's command. But if he could have used it at any time, he would've brought it out earlier.

Maybe it had to do with the Star of Bethlehem's rising.

If there was some sort of key to operating the archangel, then Kamijou might be able to stop Gabriel either by destroying the key or by taking down Fiamma himself, likely its user.

Of course, Kamijou didn't know much about the sorcery side.

However.

That doesn't matter.

As he ran, he clenched his teeth against the sounds of explosions going off in the distance.

In that case, I'll break anything I can find that seems like it might stop that angel!!

After passing through several rooms, the skies opened up.

He had reached a stone bridge with a wide path, but no railings on the sides. The gusts and explosive shock waves threatened to rock him from the side. The dark sky was murky like a midnight sea, imparting a bottomless sense of anxiety.

He didn't have time to stop for every little thing.

Even Academy City's elite units couldn't stand up to a monster like that. At this rate, they'd be conveniently used as targets for demonstration purposes. The only one with a chance of stopping that angel, even if it was indirectly, was Kamijou.

He dashed across the lengthy bridge, covering about a hundred meters in one sprint.

At what could be called the opposite shore, he opened the door to another room.

An intricate mechanism that resembled a pipe organ occupied the space here. It could have been magical in nature—or a mere decoration assembled like a puzzle. Even if it did have supernatural properties, it might not have anything to do with the angel.

Either way, checking was simple.

Kamijou only had to touch it with his right hand and see if it broke.

Decision made, he stepped deeper in the room—

"…?!"

And then caught his breath.

Right next to him. A person, hidden in some pews lined up in the room like a chapel, had suddenly tackled him from the side.

They both slammed into the floor.

The blow took Kamijou's breath away, and at first, he reflexively tried to gasp for air, but he forced the impulse down and tried to roll across the floor without breathing. If they were both down, whoever could get on top would be the winner. His assailant appeared to think the same thing; they tried to roll away as well to regain a superior position.

But the assailant banged into a pew.

Now that they had stopped, Kamijou climbed atop of the assailant.

Anyone he found here must have been an elite Roman or Russian sorcerer.

Without thinking, he got ready to bring his fist down—

"Huh…?"

—but then stopped dead.

He recognized that face.

Long, wavy blond hair hiding her eyes. Black belts that looked like physical restraints and red clothing made of a semitransparent material that looked like undergarments. She was younger than Kamijou. Hammers, saws, and a variety of other carpentry tools that had been converted into human torture implements lined the belt at her waist.

Strictly speaking, he recognized her but was not acquainted with her.

After all, the first time he'd seen her, she'd already been substituted.

He almost mixed up the names for a moment, but he managed to murmur the right one.

"Sasha Kreutzev...?"

3

Elizalina hurried through the dreary field hospital.

The fort had been used as a military facility in ages past, explaining why it only had so many windows. That said, she had already felt a disturbance before she'd peered out of one of those small portals. Still, she'd unquestionably become a witness after seeing what was happening outside, bringing unconscious words to her lips.

"This is terrible..."

Night had fallen.

A giant fortress had risen into the starless gloom, a citadel that looked like a scraped-together mess of monasteries and religious houses sourced from all over the world.

And.

Like a moon illuminating the aberrant night, something pale blue had glided through the darkness.

A human shape endowed with giant wings.

An angel.

Partially controlling an angel as telesma was one thing, but actually seeing the genuine article with the naked eye was normally unthinkable. She didn't know what Fiamma, the mastermind, was thinking, but this was an even bigger disaster than a planetoid smashing into the earth. It seemed like something that would invite an ice age upon the entire planet just to fell its enemies.

"..."

Leaning against the wall, Accelerator seemed to be watching Elizalina closely. That being said, he, too, was only here because he had been drawn to one of the few windows. Most of his thoughts were not focused on Elizalina's back but on what was happening outside.

The mysterious being, Aiwass, had told him to go to Russia.

It seemed the parchment he'd found was supposed to have been delivered to that fortress, the Russian frontline base near the national border that had risen into the air.

Then, from that fortress appeared something like *that* angel, and even now, it appeared to be launching an attack against Academy City's cream of the crop.

Yes.

An angel.

...Looks like we hit the bull's-eye. The core of the mystery, the centerpiece that got the kid and me involved in all this.

During his battle with Amata Kihara and the September 30 incident, Accelerator had witnessed a wild dance of giant wings of light. Its appearance seemed to have been related to Last Order. And using the dance of those giant wings made of light as a foundation, Aiwass had appeared.

If he was to assume that the "angel" was the same kind as the one now devastating the Russian night sky...If he was to assume that the fortress had a way of causing that angel to appear and to control it...

Then I might be able to use that technology to suppress the angel's movements or drive it away. I don't care if it's really an angel or what—this is just what the brat needed to escape her suffering!!

Elizalina, who had been watching out the window just then, suddenly turned around.

"Run away."

"What?"

"Quickly!! If you don't throw them off the trail, they'll come!!"

"Who?! Who the hell are you talking about?! And why are they after me?!"

They shouted at each other, but the first one to cool her head was Elizalina. Struggling to maintain a calm voice, she said, "...The one who instigated this war is most likely in that castle. If he can freely manipulate angels, it will be hopeless even for Academy City. If we assume their leaders properly understand the threat it poses, we'll need to consider the possibility Academy City will resort to using nuclear weapons. But..."

"But what?"

"That castle isn't complete yet." Elizalina spared another glance out the window. "The parchment you carry proves that. If those documents are so important that the mastermind Fiamma would use the army to bring them to him—if he doesn't currently have the parchment, it shows that not all the pieces have been assembled yet."

Accelerator focused his mind on the inside of his pocket where he was keeping the mysterious bundle of parchment.

"...They did go through a lot of trouble trying to deliver these in secret."

"Whatever purpose Fiamma needs to use them for, if they're necessary for his grand scheme, they will pour all their military forces into getting that last piece back...even if it means using the angel," said Elizalina slowly. "Fiamma has near complete control of Index's 103,000 volumes right now. Judging from prior examples, however, it seems possible that information regarding profoundly complex topics like angels and God's Right Seat are not recorded in those books. Perhaps that parchment's purpose is to fill those gaps in knowledge. By combining them with the 103,000 grimoires, they become a bridge to the knowledge of how to exert ultimate power and control."

"Index...?"

A slight but dangerous light went through Accelerator's eyes.

Aiwass had told him to remember the term *index of prohibited books*.

The Level Zero who had defeated Academy City's strongest Level Five had left him with the words *Index Librorum Prohibitorum*.

Here, once again, things connected—

Connected to the underworld.

And to the unknown set of rules as well, which even Accelerator didn't have a full view of, but one that definitely seemed to relate to Accelerator's and Last Order's roots.

...That piece of shit Level Zero. Exactly how many steps ahead of me is he anyway...?

Not noticing what Accelerator was thinking, Elizalina continued. "All this means you're in danger. Fiamma's followers must have reports of what the person who stole that set of parchment looks like, and unfortunately, spies had infiltrated my ranks as well. Even if you dispose of the parchment this instant, they might still capture you to find where it went."

"Like hell I'm disposing of it...," muttered Accelerator. "It could be the last key to releasing that kid from this bullshit fairy tale about angels or whatever. Even less reason for me to get rid of it."

"Then you must hurry. I'll be honest with you—if Fiamma or the Russian military gets serious, the Alliance alone can't protect you. We don't plan on going to our graves yet, so we will need to hide in order to mount an effective counterattack."

As though triggered by Elizalina's words, Accelerator looked over in another direction.

Misaka Worst was the one who responded.

"Sure thing. Misaka'll go pick up Last Order."

She waved a hand toward him. As she headed for the hospital room, she casually continued, "Still, it'd be nice to have a weapon. Even an older gun. But the rifles here have a lotta recoil, and for a shooter with one arm broken, it'd probably just be luggage, huh? Still, with only a pistol, the lack of firepower is a bit concerning— What to do, what to do? It might be because AKs come off as real strong, but does this place have any good submachine guns?"

"?" Elizalina frowned.

Ignoring her, Misaka Worst opened the door to the hospital room Last Order was in a short distance away and said, "After all, he's a big enough sucker to save Misaka. He obviously wants to show off the parchment to Russia, escape, and draw the soldiers as far away from the Alliance as possible. Eee-hee-hee."

By the time a surprised Elizalina tried to ask for details, Misaka

Worst had already gone into the medical room. Instead, the Alliance leader turned back toward Accelerator.

He was busy grating his teeth and muttering to himself. "...That bitch. That's some personality she's got. She only ever thinks of making trouble for me."

"What...? What does she mean? If what she says is true—that's far too reckless of you!!" shouted Elizalina.

Waving a hand as if to drive her away, Accelerator muttered the next thing in a short voice, like he really didn't want to.

"...Shit, it's just a little something extra, got it?"

4

A night sky, completely incongruous with the true time of day. The Star of Bethlehem, rising into the air. And an incomplete archangel, dragged from the heavens through artificial means.

William Orwell, a mercenary once called Acqua of the Back, quietly gazed upon this world in which everything was utterly twisted. After destroying the privateers' garrison base, he'd gotten partway across the snowfield toward Fiamma's fortress, but it seemed he'd been too late.

Fiamma of the Right had come this far.

Using telesma—angelic power—for personal gain was no unusual thing in modern western sorcery. But even that failed to explain the scale of this. The situation thus far had been nonsensical. Thinking about it as a technological problem, and whether one could actually do it, was nonsensical itself—but more than that, drawing out and exploiting enough power to annihilate all human life on the planet this easily was astounding.

Nevertheless.

An archangel was an archangel. While this one had announced the Son of God's inception and garnered reverence as an entity deeply involved in the birth of Crossism, it was also feared for having executed heavenly punishment upon a perverse city. It was not something even a saint, even God's Right Seat, could defeat in a head-on clash. In fact, even if all the might of humanity were arrayed on one side, it was dubious whether it could fell this archangel.

To put it briefly, that angel was strong enough to end World War III by itself.

But not through victory or defeat. The ending it offered would come after every person of every faction was slaughtered, plunging the world into a state wherein it could no longer continue the war.

I see. I can understand why Fiamma was so puffed up with pride now, admitted William Orwell honestly.

But even after the admission, his resolve would never waver.

But have you forgotten, Fiamma, what I presided over as a member of God's Right Seat?

5

Vatican City.

Cardinal Peter Iogdis moved from the center of the church toward a window. He couldn't see the situation in Russia from here. Still, even if the organization's sorcery-based monitoring was silent, reports would continue to come from his subordinates. The old man, however, ran up to the window in spite of himself. He had to—the force he'd just felt was too intense.

An efflux of divine power.

An archangel.

Gabriel.

"Ohhh…"

A noise of admiration escaped the cardinal's throat. The priests and bishops nearby, as well; some slowly made the sign of the cross, while others recited verses from the New Testament. Their great Father watched over and protected them always, but opportunities to directly sense beings this powerful were rare. The pious would find no shame in shedding tears at the event.

However.

Peter Iogdis had an entirely different feeling than the rest.

He didn't know any details about the "mastermind's" plan. They weren't collaborating, either. But he knew roughly what this Fiamma of the Right person had done. And it didn't matter what happened after this as long as it worked to Peter Iogdis's benefit.

In other words.

If he could use this opportunity to seize the papal throne.

He considered secretly communicating with a bishop of the Russian Church— Was it because their circumstances had many commonalities?

...I was somewhat impatient while chasing the activity records of Academy City forces in Russia, but— Why, this means our victory is assured! The papal conclave is about to convene as well, just as I suspected. I can become the one who leads this world as the next pope!!

He'd heard that signs of riots were visible all over Italy, but the cardinal didn't care about that. The sudden change in scenery from day to night would probably deepen the chaos already going on. Just as the existence of Halley's Comet had once caused societal unrest. But that wasn't relevant. The Roman Orthodox Church had dispatched agents into the the general populace to make sure their riots stayed within acceptable levels, and even if that didn't grant them complete control, there were other, more important things to focus on. First came strengthening his own position. Peter Iogdis would deploy Roman Orthodox forces to pacify the people after that. Then there wouldn't be any problems. He'd keep damages at a tolerable level, and by the time they'd finished dealing with the debris and the dead bodies, Peter Iogdis would have ascended to the position closest to the Lord in this world.

However.

"Cardinal Peter Iogdis!!"

All of a sudden, an armed priest—someone unfit for this place— burst inside.

"It's an emergency!! They're temporarily suspending the conclave! We will shore up the defenses, so please, retreat deeper inside!!"

"..."

His feathers ruffled. From his spot next to the window, Peter Iogdis lowered his gaze to the ground. The city of Rome wasn't visible over the thick intervening wall, but he could hear what sounded like a tumult.

It was, in fact, an uproarious riot, and he found himself seething that the filthy rabble should have just stayed inside Rome for their violence. But they seemed to have changed directions and gone toward the Vatican. It appeared that those Roman Orthodox agents he'd placed in the populace hadn't been enough to suppress them after all.

"The papal conclave will proceed as scheduled."

"B-but, sir!!"

"Use the Roman Orthodox forces to suppress them. A baptism of blood will silence the unwashed masses. They cannot be allowed to overturn the great things we are performing."

"We can't!! That order causes a contradiction with our chain of command!! We have been allowed to strengthen our defenses to prepare for any incidents, but we can't take offensive action against them!!"

"What?" said Peter Iogdis, his face clouding over.

The priest's answer was incomprehensible to him. With the Roman pope currently absent, Peter Iogdis and the other cardinals were the church's highest authorities. And out of the many cardinals, he possessed the greatest authority. That meant that when it came to *public* strength, the orders of Peter Iogdis were absolute.

But the armed priest wouldn't obey them.

He explained:

"It's the Roman pope…"

It sounded like he'd squeezed the words out.

And yet, it also sounded like somewhere inside, he'd been waiting for this.

"Our Roman pope has calmed the riotous masses with a mere few words!! He is now entering the country! We don't have any way to stop his advance!!"

The Roman pope.

What he had done in the streets hadn't been anything special. He simply spoke to everyone, approaching them, listening to what they had to say, and taking the time to soothe their rattled nerves.

That was all.

Normally, a crowd close to fifty thousand on the verge of a riot might have beaten him to a pulp. And they might have even taken his words and actions as the spark that would ignite a devastating explosion.

In spite of all that, even with their unique group psychology that had become so strangely intense, the kind that treated fighting to be the natural course during war and would assume anyone standing still at such a time was evil—at his words, everyone regained their humanity. The pope hadn't produced any magical effects to sway their emotions, nor had he read out a speech carefully composed to sway those caught up in mob mentality. The words of this one old man just slowly permeated everyone's thoughts and spread, causing one person, then another, to lower their guns or blades.

Of course...

It wasn't as though the world could be fully related to a simple scale of good and evil. Some of those in the crowds were Roman Orthodox agents, who purposely wanted to incite riots. They weren't aiming for complete anarchy, but they were more wary of the people being quietly absorbed into supporting the Roman pope. Because of that, some tried to use a single gunshot to overturn their disadvantageous situation. By provoking a throng of people that straddled the line between chaos and stability, the agents were hoping to cause an even stronger outburst. In times like these, it was simpler to induce a great panic with an easily understood gunshot than by using strange sorcery. Those from the Roman Orthodox Church had written the book on how to manipulate the enormous group of two billion faithful—they'd assumed a single gunshot would be more than enough.

And yet.

I can't...

The professional assassin couldn't reach into his pocket. Nobody could bring themselves to fire on the pope of Rome, who had calmed so many people and who said he would set things right on his own.

Deep inside him was terror.

Leaden pressure had gone to the pit of his stomach, and it had frozen this true assassin's hands.

This terror, however, was a peculiar fear that assassins, who had killed and killed so many times, had never before tasted.

I can't allow the small thing this man is creating to end, no matter what...!!

And thus, the pope's advance began.

Many stood in his way: assassins both easily spotted and well hidden. But the pope of Rome never said a word. He didn't brace himself. He simply continued forward. That was all it took for everyone to yield and make a path, convincing them to drop their weapons and Soul Arms and even inducing some among them to cry and repent. Before anyone knew it, many were following in the wake of his advance. These weren't people whose minds were consumed by whirling emotions like passion—it was a simple, quiet procession.

The armed priests who had been defending the main gate at the Vatican City border quietly crossed themselves at the pope's return.

Some even said aloud that they hoped things would turn for the better.

The old man continued forth.

Each one of his steps represented mankind's resistance to the great monster known as global warfare.

This was a battle that would test their worth as people—armed not with swords and guns but with reason and compassion.

"...No..."

Upon seeing the old man enter the church's front entrance, Peter Iogdis shook his head.

His expression resembled that of a child on the verge of tears.

"No!!!!!! I am...the next pope—it's going to be me!! The decision was already made!! You're nothing more than a ghost! You have no more place here!! K-kill him. The chaos currently gripping the Roman Orthodox Church is all this monster's fault!! If I become pope, I promise you all lives many times more prosperous!! So kill hiiiiiiiiiiiiiiiiiiiiiiiiiiiiiiiiiiiiiiiiiiiiiiiiiiiiiiiiiiim!!"

"..."

"What are you doing?! Warrior—for what purpose did we give you spears?! To pierce the enemy!! And skewer all the foolish masses who obey him!! You must do it!! That is the only way for me to preside over this world!!"

"Do not fear."

A grave, elderly voice quieted Peter's apparent temper tantrum for a moment.

"I do not intend to stop you if you wish to hold the papal conclave. If you would demand that someone must bear the responsibility for the chaos in the Roman Orthodox Church, I would even consider heading for the gallows. I am no longer the pope of Rome. I am but a single believer, Matthew Reese, and I come before you today to bring an end to this war."

"Wh...what...?"

"In the basement of St. Peter's Cathedral, half destroyed by Fiamma's hand, was a grand storehouse boasting such vast knowledge that we invited the British-made index of prohibited books to it. I am going to peruse that knowledge. A plan for combating Fiamma's sanctuary may yet sleep within it."

Finished, Matthew Reese stepped forward.

Peter Iogdis withdrew like a magnet of the same charge. But he soon hit a wall. As he continued to shake his head, the old man drew closer.

I'll be killed.

That thought naturally rose to the core of his mind. It only made sense, considering what he'd done until now. Matthew Reese held no weapon or Soul Arm, but that wasn't comforting in the slightest. Peter Iogdis knew of the man's skill in sorcery—and even without using it, a single command would be enough for the people, the armed priests, the bishops, and everyone else to lose themselves and rend Peter Iogdis asunder. When all was said and done, he had no true allies.

And yet.

With a *pat*, Matthew Reese placed a hand on Peter Iogdis's shoulder. It was a gentle gesture. Then, the man who had given up his papal throne said this to the man who had tried to steal it:

"You've done well shepherding two billion followers in such difficult times. Your talent is unquestionably the reason everyone here has survived while I was asleep. As you say, I am an incompetent leader. Alone, I would likely have allowed the damage to grow even further."

He was smiling.

It was neither an act to deceive nor a distorted grin of sarcasm or derision. Matthew Reese, now no more than another believer, had just blessed Peter Iogdis's progress from the bottom of his heart.

"Please, call me when the papal conclave commences. I will cast my vote for you. You have borne the brunt of the criticism, performed many decisions of authority, and protected the lives of everyone—you deserve praise for that much, at least. It may not be much, but please, allow me to aid you on the path you walk."

Saying only that, Matthew Reese turned about.

"Do you understand? We are fighting so you can survive. Promise me you will not die before this war ends."

Matthew Reese had abandoned his position as pope—and yet, when Peter Iogdis looked at the man's reassuring back, it seemed to him as though it contained everything he had ever desired.

Unable even to see the one old man off as he went, pressed onward to a new battlefield to fight for what he believed in, Peter Iogdis, whose only labors had been in search of wealth, broke down into tears.

6

"Sasha Kreutzev…?" murmured Touma Kamijou, still straddling her.

His thoughts weren't coming together.

The archangel called Misha Kreutzev was, even as he spoke, flying in the artificial night sky, trying to crush Academy City's forces.

But Sasha Kreutzev was right here before his eyes.

The blond-haired girl, slight body tightened with clothing that looked like physical restraints, tilted her head a little and asked, "Question one. Why do you know my name?"

"Where to start…Uh, we actually met one time at the end of August, but strictly speaking, that was Misha Kreutzev, and we've never spoken to each other directly, but I heard from Kanzaki and Tsuchimikado that the original body before the substitution belonged to Sasha Kreutzev—"

"…"

Before he could finish, Sasha twisted and turned, throwing Kamijou wide, the boy who was leaning over her. He gave a startled grunt, and she looked at him with suspicious eyes behind her bangs.

"Answer one. I have judged that I will not get a good explanation from you. As an addendum, I estimate the probability that you are an enemy, given that you are on board this Star of Bethlehem, to be extremely high. Are you part of their team, come to apprehend me for fleeing the ritual site?"

Shweeng!! She pulled a saw and an L-shaped pair of pincers from her waist belt.

The blood drained from Kamijou's face. "Whoa!! You're like this whether you're Misha or Sasha?! What the hell is that angel anyway?! Is it *really* unrelated to you?!"

As Kamijou, in a panic, scrambled to speak, Sasha fell silent for a moment. Like a cautious beast, she inched away a few steps, thinking, *…This man still seems suspicious nevertheless, but he also appears to know something about my "condition"…*

What tugged at her was the *end of August* part.

That was right around when Sasha had acquired the strange condition. It allowed her to feel a pressure in her chest whenever someone else's mana or a Soul Arm was nearby. According to the Russian Catholic analysis team, she showed signs of having had immense power inside her on an archangelic level, but…

She glanced at the torture saw...*I can force him to speak now, but I can't tell whether this man is a simple idiot or if he's being intentionally dense. Perhaps a shorter route to the correct answer would be to not clearly and straightforwardly ask him.*

As Sasha quietly decided on a new course of action, Kamijou asked, "Do you know a man named Fiamma of the Right? He's supposed to be the guy who kidnapped you from the Elizalina Alliance of Independent Nations and brought you here."

"...?"

"He's gotta be doing something." Kamijou glanced toward the door of the stone-built room. "Otherwise, that monster wouldn't have shown up. Fiamma called you a *medium for the angel* or something. I'll be direct: He used you to summon that angel, didn't he?"

Angel summoning.

Calling it that might have made it sound ridiculous, but Kamijou knew firsthand how fearsome it was. Both in terms of sorcery, from the Angel Fall incident at the end of August, and in terms of science, from the events surrounding Fuse Kazakiri that took place on September 30.

What Fiamma had done was equally threatening. But at the same time, Kamijou also thought that angels weren't the kind of thing that could be controlled so easily. There had to be groundwork. The groundwork was for the Angel Fall magic circle for Misha Kreutzev and the AIM dispersion fields for Fuse Kazakiri. Whatever was happening, it was being supported by some large-scale mechanism, and if that was removed, they'd be unable to move, at least, in this world.

He knew what the key was this time.

Sasha Kreutzev.

If a prodigious angel had appeared with her at the origin, then Sasha might have been in contact with some sort of important Soul Arm. It was an assumption that something like that even existed, but that meant Sasha might know what he should destroy to disable the angel.

"Listen. Tell me whatever you might know. First, where in the Star of Bethlehem did Fiamma use his magic to summon the angel—the ritual, I guess you'd call it in this case? Anyway, I want you to show me where the action happened. Also, it would be great to hear about the process, even if you only know a rough outline. I want to know what kind of tools he used at the time, and how."

Naturally, Kamijou didn't know sorcery. But his right hand didn't care whether he understood the underlying principles—his ability could erase and destroy any phenomena or object related to the supernatural. If he busted up every single thing she mentioned, it might lead to destroying Misha.

Sasha still seemed to be suspicious of Kamijou after he suddenly asked all that at once.

But even at this moment, the archangel was flying about in the skies, launching huge attacks at Academy City aircraft and the Russian surface—she could tell by the faint rumbling. They had a common interest, and that connection made Sasha start to murmur.

"...Answer two. When I woke up, the ritual was already over. Maybe that was why I was able to escape. Many Russian sorcerers were around other than the mastermind, so under normal circumstances, I wouldn't have been able to flee all the way here. To be blunt, when they relaxed just for a moment after the hard part was over, I took advantage of it and ran out of the ritual site."

"That's fine. Did you see anything in the ritual site before you ran away?"

Would Fiamma allow an opening that easily? And how could you even *run* from Fiamma, who could travel miles in a single instant? Kamijou was privately dubious, but he didn't mention it now. Maybe he'd just decided she had nowhere to run, locked up on a fortress high in the skies.

Sasha, for her part, seemed to notice what he was thinking and continued the technical explanation. "Answer three. The ritual site was of the Crossist format. It had an odd construction, intensively using fire in particular out of the four aspects...Normally, excluding extreme usage as a means of attack, ritual sites only gain significance after bringing all four aspects together as one. But that man called Fiamma—his ritual site was far too unified in a single color..."

Kamijou abruptly looked at his right hand. Maybe...

...there was another way.

Fiamma had used Sasha to summon that archangel. This time, instead of it residing inside Sasha like during Angel Fall, the archangel was pure—and exposed to the open air. On the other hand, if he'd used Sasha to summon Misha, it was highly likely the same logic was being applied here. Sasha was still necessary to stabilize the archangel's existence.

In that case, maybe Sasha and Misha were connected, like with an out-of-body experience. If so, Kamijou could use the Imagine Breaker. By touching Sasha, he might deal direct damage to Misha. After all, angels were apparently big clusters of magical energy.

...While we're standing around, Misha Kreutzev is wrecking the entire area. Academy City and Russian forces are one thing, but the damage could have even spread to civilian homes already.

Kamijou opened and closed his right hand.

Which means the only thing I can do is test everything I can. Here and now, we're the only ones who can act!!

"As an addendum, regarding the ritual site's location...When observing the fortress's direction of motion, it should be located at the rightmost tip of the Star of Bethlehem. Here, too, he is probably trying to take advantage of the sign of the angel Michael, who symbolizes fire. His methods are thorough, but on the other hand, the angel floating around the battlefield now is Gabriel, which symbolizes water—and on that point, I feel a strong sense of strangeness— *Hyawaah?!*"

Sasha abruptly straightened up and let out a yelp.

Kamijou's right hand had reached for her cheek.

Not noticing how she was trembling, he repeatedly pressed his hand to her head, then shoulders, side, stomach, and thigh.

"...Not here. Not here, either—or here or here. Damn it—no

change in Misha. Maybe this won't work. I'll just check the back first. I gotta say, these are some ridiculous clothes…"

"…"

While Kamijou murmured to himself, Sasha, without a word, swung around her L-shaped crowbar.

Ba-gam!! She struck him with the back of the weapon, cleanly in the temple.

"…Question two. Are you of the same mind as Vasilisa?"

"*Grbhhh?!* What—? *Kfht!* What's a Vasilisa?!" shouted Kamijou faintly from the floor, limbs twitching.

Sasha swung down the crowbar's right-angle section a few more times, but then, apparently deciding beating him to a pulp wouldn't improve the situation, she went bright red in the face and put the torture device back on her belt for the time being.

"Answer four. The man named Fiamma's ritual site was of high grade, but the Soul Arms he used himself were commonplace ones. Not the sort that should give him the power to control an angel of that magnitude."

…Maybe the special-made tool in this case was Sasha herself, and he only needed tools of normal capabilities to draw out hers.

"However, as an addendum, there was one Soul Arm I'd never seen before."

"A Soul Arm?!"

Kamijou jumped at that without thinking.

Maybe it was related to the Soul Arm that remotely controlled Index.

"Answer five. In concrete terms, it was a staff. Actually, the symbolic weapon of fire is a rod or a staff, so that isn't strange, per se."

"Why'd it catch your attention, then?"

"As an addendum, a staff as the Symbolic Weapon of fire is completed by inserting a bar magnet into the end of its red-painted body. But his staff wasn't like that."

"?"

"As a further addendum, to specify, it was a cylinder about this big, small enough to fit in your palm, and it had several small rings on the side. It looked similar to a dial padlock. He'd embedded that in the tip of his staff."

"…"

He had an idea what that Soul Arm was.

The one that could remotely control Index.

Had Fiamma used the knowledge in the 103,000 grimoires in his ritual to summon Misha Kreutzev? For a moment, he thought so, but then he realized something didn't make sense about Sasha's explanation.

Fiamma had been controlling Index just by using the Soul Arm in his hand. He would have been able to draw the necessary knowledge from her.

Why would he have had to modify it, then embed it as part of a staff?

Kamijou thought for a moment, then murmured, "…Wait, you mean he's applying the Soul Arm's effect—to manipulate others from a distance—in order to control Misha Kreutzev…?"

7

"We're on the counterattack at last…," murmured Nikolai Tolstoj, Russian bishop, in a palace in Moscow.

He was holding a communication Soul Arm shaped like a book.

Right now, it was connected to Fiamma.

"We saw Misha Kreutzev's emergence from here as well. I'm surprised you were able to amass that much telesma in one place. As long as we can use it as a combat force, nothing else matters. I'll have you help us crush Academy City's forces at once."

Nikolai had several other maps and documents spread out on the table aside from the communication Soul Arm.

"Most of their forces consist of unmanned weapons, a mixture of AI and remote control. We'll start by destroying their command center here. Our first priority is to win on the EU front that's steadily approaching Moscow from eastern Europe. Once that's over, we eliminate the airborne forces passing over the Arctic Sea. I'll send you maps and their unit movements. Waste no time when you get them—"

"Heh-heh."

Then it happened.

Nikolai was sure he'd just heard Fiamma laugh.

"*It may be incomplete, but I have the archangel of water under my full control—and all you can think of is trivial nonsense.*"

"What…are you saying?"

"*I understand why you capped out as a bishop. The world is full of incongruity, but this, perhaps, was correct. The office of Patriarch doesn't suit you. The organization would doubtless begin to collapse.*"

"What are you saying, Fiamma?!"

His position—his complex—attacked, Nikolai flew into a rage.

But nothing changed. Fiamma of the Right only continued to laugh.

"*Let me ask you something, Nikolai. Did you think I would spend my personal wealth for Russia's sake? Of course not. Not even if the opposite happened.*"

"You…little…"

"*I use my wealth for my own, much greater purposes. Why don't we sum this up? You've done well buying me time, reverent Bishop Nikolai Tolstoj. A low role such as that suits you. Fight with Academy City on your own now—and be destroyed on your own.*"

"Heh…"

Nikolai's emotions exploded.

But it wasn't anger.

It was joy—joy that what he'd prepared for this moment hadn't gone to waste.

"You're an imbecile, Fiamma!! You are wrong about the most fundamental thing! Have you forgotten the Russian spells embedded in the fortress you personally lifted into the sky?!"

"…"

"The two hundred sorcerers I dispatched there are all working for me. Did you think I wouldn't plant anything? One order from me, and that fortress will fall apart in the blink of an eye, raining back down upon the earth as so many random items."

In exchange for the ability to use special sorcery normal people couldn't, those in God's Right Seat couldn't use magic normal sorcerers could. That was why Fiamma had asked for sorcerer aid from the Russian Church. In other words, normal spells were absolutely indispensable for that fortress's structure.

And.

The same went for removing Nikolai's trap, laid secretly within the spell that had constructed the fortress.

"What now, Fiamma?" demanded Nikolai. He had always made his fortune off of profiteering during wartime—he was used to deals like these. "I don't know what you're trying to use that fortress for, but if you were that thorough in your preparations to lift it up, it must be essential to your plans. Do you want me to destroy it?"

I've won, thought Nikolai.

He'd completely grasped the initiative.

"If you follow the will of Russia, I won't need to dismantle that fortress. Come—it's a simple matter of priorities, Fiamma. Russia comes first. If we have time after that, you can execute your objectives. As long as that doesn't cause issues for Russia."

"*Ha-ha.*"

He heard Fiamma laugh quietly.

Nikolai frowned. That wasn't what he'd expected.

It wasn't a self-deprecating laugh, one with resignation in it. Fiamma's laugh was real, as though someone had just told him an awful joke.

In other words.

He was laughing *at* him.

"*If that is truly the deepest plot you can think of, then even a bishopric was too much for you.*"

A moment later.

A *criiick*, like something tearing apart a fiber, rang in Nikolai's ears. Instantly, a bad feeling swept through him. A magical line necessary for dismantling the fortress's construction spell had been severed.

"A mere part of God's Right Seat can't use normal magic. You are right on that point—but it would be illogical. Why do you think I invaded the UK to obtain the Soul Arm to remotely control the 103,000 volumes?"

"You…No…"

His throat dried up.

He thought he'd had the initiative, and now it was slipping through his fingers like a healthy fish.

"Of the four aspects, I command fire—but not only fire. The four aspects lie at the ends of their own directions. Manipulating one aspect can be interpreted loosely as affecting the other three as well. I have everything I need in order to use sorcery."

"Use it…? You have power other than God's Right Seat—? No!!"

"Still, I should detach in order to become the kami-jo. But the usage is what's important. I can amass the knowledge of man through prudent, appropriate usage. Of course, when all is completed, the sacred light will inevitably eliminate the petty darkness known as human knowledge.

"*What I'm trying to say is this*," Fiamma finished quietly, as if to deal the finishing blow to the shallow bishop:

"I requested sorcerers to gain the necessary information about the spells—and to let the Russians slip into negligence. Unfortunately for you, your role is at an end. That last lifeline you were clinging to has just now broken. And I'll deal with the two hundred sorcerers on my end. Anyway—Well, don't worry about it. Just die in whatever way you please."

The communication ended.

It had been a one-sided fight.

He felt as though the difference in their worth to the world had been made palpable. One was the leader of God's Right Seat, in control of the world's fate. The other was a single dime-a-dozen bishop.

For a time, Nikolai Tolstoj contemplated his mortality…until his anger fully erupted.

He shoved the book-shaped communication Soul Arm off the table and grabbed a cell phone. It had an encrypted communication chip for high-ranking government officials embedded in it, and with it, he gave an order to another subordinate.

"Send in the *reserves*."

The word had a terrifying meaning within it.

He simply shouted, ignoring even how big of a crisis his command would place Russia in.

"I want that fortress blown up!! *Right now!!*"

8

The battle between Index and Stiyl was still raging in St. George's Cathedral.

Unfortunately, that battle wasn't even close to a true contest.

Stiyl, a mere sorcerer, and the grimoire library freely controlling its stock of 103,000 volumes would never have been an even match.

"Chapter thirteen, verse nine. Executing preservation of reach via projectiles."

Bang!! The red wings on Index's back burst off.

The red light, like blood splattering, shot at Stiyl like a laser. It would be more than one or two—dozens of attacks were coming at him all at once, from all different angles.

"...!!"

Stiyl didn't die instantly, partly because of the location.

Part of the floor on the ground level had collapsed, so Stiyl and Index had fallen into the underground Soul Arm storehouse.

He grabbed a Soul Arm at once, fed mana into it, and activated it.

The block-shaped stone, dubbed the Stone of Hrungnir, glowed with a pale-blue hue, then successfully repelled four of the red lights Index had fired.

All of the rest rushed at him, destroying the Soul Arm along with its pale-blue light.

Twisting himself, Stiyl barely avoided the lethal rays.

...From what I can see, the physical control itself uses her brain.

The remote-control Soul Arm is only sending her the necessary signals—the parameters needed for actions use what's inside her already. Which means if I can knock Index out, she'll stop.

It pained him to put any more of a burden on her, but it was his only choice. He checked the runic cards in his clothes. They weren't only flames. He had many other cards ready that could produce other effects, centered around Opila to drive others away. Depending on how he combined them, he could create a myriad of effects, and among them was one to mentally bind a targeted person.

He'd postponed doing this because he couldn't predict the risk—he didn't know how compatible it would be with the remote-control Soul Arm—but he didn't have any more time to hesitate. He would swiftly disable Index and mentally restrain her.

The issue was...

How am I supposed to get close to her under this continuous barrage?!

That was when a huge *ba-boom* went off.

It was the sound of the door to the basement Soul Arm storehouse flying open and several Sisters stepping inside.

"Stiyl, we're here to assist!! Please regroup—"

"Stop!!"

By the time Stiyl shouted in reply, it was too late.

"Chapter eight, verse forty-three. Mana refinement detected. Identifying those drawing power as hostile entities and eliminating their ability to act."

Pop. Sparks appeared near Index's brow.

Immediately after, a large, fan-shaped shock wave billowed out from Index. It knocked over all the Sisters, who were most likely protected to an extent with Soul Arms, then destroyed an entire wall of the underground Soul Arm storehouse before carrying the hostile parties far away like a bulldozer.

Our main combat personnel are all deployed at the Strait of Dover and overseas. Most of the people remaining here are for communication and correspondence. At this rate, she'll wipe us out!!

Index's head twisted to look around.

Detecting mana in the walls, the ceiling…and beyond them, she said, "Chapter eight, verse forty-seven. Continuing to eliminate factors with high probability of becoming hostile."

Boom!! Bang!! One after another, thick beam-looking things fired out. They easily penetrated the walls and ceiling, guarded by magical barriers, then continued, destroying one of St. George's Cathedral's magical mechanisms after the next.

Not good. At this rate, she might affect the large-scale Soul Arms supporting our forces on the front lines!!

Then it happened: Someone walked up to the edge of where the ceiling had collapsed.

It was Laura Stuart, archbishop and leader of the English Puritan Church.

…Reinforcements…? he wondered in slight anticipation before realizing he was wrong a moment later.

She shook her hand, displaying something.

As if to show it off.

That's…her remote-control Soul Arm!!

She was far from reinforcements.

Her silent gesture meant something very simple.

Do something quickly, or I'll use this.

Stiyl clenched his teeth.

Index was clearly already under massive strain. It was easy to see what would happen if that woman used her remote-control Soul Arm on top of everything else.

He removed runic cards from his inside pocket and forced mana through them.

A sword of flames appeared.

Index's eyes turned his way, as if drawn to it.

"Chapter twenty, verse six. Reestablishing priority targets. Reevaluation of dangerous factors complete."

After waiting for her to have her attention on him, Stiyl dashed to the exit of the underground Soul Arm storehouse. If they stayed here, it would only increase the damage. For now, he had to start by luring her into an optimal battlefield.

As Stiyl withdrew, the girl's unfeeling voice followed after him.

"Preparations complete. Commencing attack."

INTERLUDE
FIVE

On the white snowfield, Mikoto Misaka looked overhead.

It seemed like the giant fortress with that spiky-haired boy on it was still floating, even now. She'd come all this way to Russia, but at this rate, no matter how long she waited, she'd never reach him.

...Come on!! I came all the way here to be left out in the cold?! That's not possible!! I have to think of some way to get to him!!

No matter how she thought about it, that spiky-haired boy was at the dead center of this disturbance. Being positioned in the middle of World War III made her wonder how much bigger things were for that idiot, but she could lecture him on his foolishness after she'd dragged him somewhere safe.

And then the Sister next to her offered, "What in the world is that frog strap hanging out of your jacket pocket, asks Misaka, brimming with curiosity."

"Eh? He's called Croaker. I got it from the cell phone campaign when I dragged that idiot there on September 30."

"...First, Misaka number 10032's necklace, and now this strap... The girls in Academy City certainly seem to have the advantage, says Misaka, implying a rethinking of her strategy. Boy, being long-distance is tough."

"Er, what strategy?"

Mikoto blinked in confusion, but the Sister, hugging her Russian assault rifle like a stuffed animal, didn't provide any further answers.

She glanced above, toward the fortress. "I would like to somehow support him, says Misaka, presenting an impossible problem."

"...Same, but the issue is how exactly we'll get there. It's probably gone up five thousand meters, yeah? Not even my magnetism can reach that far."

"Would it be possible to increase your altitude in stages by preparing several relay points in midair? asks Misaka, haphazardly suggesting an idea."

"How would we do that?" asked Mikoto.

The Sister took a look around, then pointed to a Russian short-range missile launcher mounted onto a vehicle. "First, we'll fire one of those missiles—"

"I'll die!" interrupted Mikoto, rejecting it. "But a regular military helicopter wouldn't reach that high, either. It's not airtight, and the fortress looks like it's still rising. If we really want to go, I guess we'll need a plane..."

"(...Appearing gallantly when it should be utterly impossible to do so might be my biggest chance to overturn my long-distance handicap, says Misaka, with a low laugh, beginning to discharge devious fantasies into the network.)"

"Hey, you're leaking something, you know," said Mikoto, appalled.

But then, the Sister's face quickly rose.

Partially attentive to her wireless headset device, she said, "I've intercepted a Russian communication, reports Misaka. The encryption format is different from regular military correspondences. The name Nikolai Tolstoj appears multiple times; it must be from some sort of independent unit, estimates Misaka."

"?"

"They seem to be on the verge of launching a large-scale attack from the ground against the fortress floating in the air, says Misaka, summarizing the essential details."

"Hmm. That's not good. That would mean that idiot up there would get caught in it."

She didn't honestly care what happened to that strange fortress, but even she'd have a bad aftertaste if an acquaintance of hers blew up along with it. It was important to find a way to get to the fortress overhead, but maybe she needed to stop the attack from the surface first.

"So—what weapons are they going to use? They've been firing short-range surface-to-air missiles for a while now, but it doesn't seem like they'll even dent it."

"Nu-AD1967."

"What's that?"

"The American name for it, says Misaka, continuing her explanation. Apparently, it is referred to here as *Opasnosti*, says Misaka, listening to the communication."

"What does that all mean?"

"A strategic nuclear warhead developed by the old Soviet Union, reports Misaka."

CHAPTER 8

Their Multilateral Counterattack
Combination.

1

Misha Kreutzev.

The size of the angel's body by itself wasn't that unusual. Two meters, give or take. Perhaps its consistently feminine silhouette was because this being stood as the only female angel in legend.

The details of the angel's form, however, were clearly distinct from humans.

Instead of skin, a silky fabric covered its body; and it had no face to speak of—no eyes, nose, or mouth. Those organs were all depicted solely by unevenness in the cloth. In place of its hair was a cloth spread in the shape of a trumpet, flowing from the back of its head.

No strict distinction could be made between skin and cloth; they were one and the same. Gold-colored veins, like that of a leaf, ran through the white cloth's surface, held in some places by pins of the same color. On the whole, it was closer to a white or gray, but the faint-blue light emanating from its body caused its impression to morph into something more radiant.

Its wings were ice.

They numbered around a hundred.

Their sizes were anywhere from a dozen inches or so to three hundred feet.

The countless wings, towering like a massive pin frog turned to the heavens, possessed a beauty unique to crystalline structures. A gemstone beauty, one which would confront any who tried to reproduce it with the disparity between them and nature.

However.

Those from Academy City, their units deployed across Russian lands, could not watch in fascination.

They knew of its horrors.

No—they were forced to know.

Roar!!!!!!
The countless wings of ice caused the snowy lands to shake.

The action Misha had taken had been simple.

It had descended, straight down, from the air to the center of the tightly clustered, tank- and powered suit–laden enemy ranks. During its meteoric impact, it swung its three-digit wings protruding from its back wildly down in all directions.

That was all.

With no more than a giant stamping-like movement, the Academy City teams who had been sweeping through the huge nation of Russia were scattered like an ant line trampled on by a child.

"Whoooooooooaaaaaaa?!"

"Get away from it! It's too close for bombardment!!"

"Does it look like we have time for that?!"

As the tanks retreated with enough force they nearly ran over their allied powered suits, they rotated their turrets with precision.

Fire spewed from their muzzles.

With the organ-scrambling *boom* of their bombardment, the artillery, made to dig deep inside armor before igniting, ripped through the air.

The angel didn't even turn its head.

Its wings, giant as steel towers, simply swung—faster than the speed of sound, stirring the atmosphere, and even leaving trails of condensation in their wakes. With overwhelming force, the unleashed wing attack easily shot down the paltry tank shells.

There was no counterattack.

To begin with, Misha hadn't even viewed this action as a hostile one with a winner and a loser.

"anhwrNEXTnxdp"

By the time anyone had heard the *bang*, Misha's body had already soared up thirty thousand feet into the air.

Academy City's unit deployment spanned far more than merely three hundred feet.

Misha set its sights on its next landing point, away from the crater in the crowd.

A moment later.

In the same way as before, Misha Kreutzev plunged straight toward the middle of a unit.

"nipsergNEXTnsig"

"sbrgNEXTsnmtph"

"nithgNEXTgbsvrfl"

Bang!! Boom!! In rapid succession, Academy City units were gouged and hollowed. It wasn't certain whether Misha had a sense of friend or foe. Brought into the melee, the Russian tanks and armored vehicles moving about in confusion were mowed down at the same time.

It was an overpowering sight to behold.

The Academy City tank crewmen crawling out of their tanks, which were now like shredded empty cans, locked eyes with the sunken Russian troops then. But they never pointed their muzzles at one another's chests. The Russian troops simply shook their heads in dumb amazement. The Academy City tank crewmen could understand how they felt.

This was far more than a war now.

Even the act of war was nothing but part of a life cycle that humans had created between themselves.

This was a true catastrophe.

And faced with that, human agency had no way to continue.

"hbsugzevnzfNEXTsboisngrger"

Words, sent forth.

A language indiscernible to the human ear, incomprehensible to the human mind.

The soldiers looked to the skies, feeling like blade tips had been thrust at their throats. The angel of destruction reigned supreme. Misha's movements didn't change. And it never altered its method of attack on a whim. Did it feel like this was a tedious job? An instant after Misha's face pointed in their direction, its body had slammed into them like a meteor, without hesitation.

They were done for next time.

It was a miracle they'd lived this long.

Their luck had hit rock bottom.

"…"

Energy drained from the Academy City tank crewmen, and for some reason, smiles came to their lips.

The Russian troops were probably making the same kind of expression.

And a moment later, the archangel descended.

Without mercy.

To grant death to all living things.

Boom!! echoed an explosion.

However—it was not the sound of Misha Kreutzev making landfall.

It was the sound of someone colliding with the archangel in midair.

Neither the Academy City tank crews nor the Russian troops understood what had just happened. Their state of confusion was so stunning that it took them time to even realize the simple fact that their lives still continued on.

A woman had clashed with the archangel.

A blond-haired woman, wearing a dress that was red like burning fire, holding a sword of flashing light in her right hand.

Despite her location three hundred meters aboveground—a clear departure from the range of motion a simple human was supposed to be capable of—the woman, shot at her target like a rocket, had clashed one-on-one with the archangel.

For the first time, Misha's trajectory deviated.

Losing most of its force and speed, Misha Kreutzev's body, its trajectory forced into a sideways slide, thrust toward the ground—not vertically but at an angle. This time, no crater was created. Bouncing a few times, Misha stabbed its ice wings into the ground to force itself to stop. It was evident that troops from both armies were hastily moving away from the archangel's surroundings.

What was that?

What happened?

One of the Academy City tank crewmen was rattled, but he neither had time to think deeply nor settle his mind. The woman in the red dress who had exchanged blows with Misha in the skies landed right next to the tank crewman.

Without using a parachute or anything.

With only her two feet, she floated down.

"Ah, ah, whooaa?!"

The tank crewman, fallen on his rear end, tried to get away, but the woman paid no attention to him. She only gave a shake of her sword made of flashing light and glanced toward the archangel.

At the horror that he didn't want to place in his field of vision, even for an instant.

"…Seriously. Even these so-called heavenly gofers are basically just monsters like this, so. I thought I'd get an earful of all sorts of heaven's secrets considering she's the angel of the Enunciation, but we can't even speak to each other."

Her voice was plainly scornful.

In addition.

"If you are anything of a nation's princess, why not have a little more restraint? ...Although I suppose I have no right to criticize now that you've persuaded me to come to a place even Napoleon grew sick and tired of."

What?! ...What—? When did she show up?!

The tank crewman, who turned around after perceiving another woman's voice, then noticed for the first time the pallid woman wearing a loose-fitting outfit of white cloth.

But that wasn't all.

"Even still, ma'am, the idea of you exchanging blows in these conditions makes this a grave situation. It does indeed seem that the enemy has prepared something with purity equaling—or even exceeding—the Curtana."

This time, it was a man's voice. There, behind a man wearing an expensive-looking suit, waited hundreds, if not thousands, of people. It was unbelievable. Sure, there were a few hills and valleys here and there—but it was basically flatland here. There were no obstacles that could hide this many people. And despite that...

But it didn't seem like this situation was something he could ask the details of from the woman in the red dress, the pallid woman, or the man in the suit.

They exchanged words with cool expressions.

"I figure your weapon nullification spell doesn't work?"

"Unfortunately no, ma'am. This is far beyond its level. And it may be that those wings are being perceived not as weapons, but as part of its body."

"What is Necessarius doing anyway? Can't we use that saint they have?"

"They seem to be prioritizing medical aid for the wounded, for both Academy City and the Russian forces. For her, it seems battle is but one means of salvation, and other methods were higher on her priority list."

Carissa tisked softly at the Knight Leader's words.

The Femme Fatale's eyebrow twitched. "That seems the proper response for the Puritans, no?" Ignoring the glare the second princess cast on her, the French holy woman continued. "In the first place, that department has been killing far too much."

"Don't need you to tell me that," muttered Carissa. "Hmph. That means I'll just have to manage with *this*."

Voom!! She swung the sword of flashing light once.

Then she turned toward the woman with the sickly looking skin, who gripped a sword adorned with decorations, and said, "You good, Frenchy?"

"I don't know why you're asking me when you're the one who fiddled with the mobile fortress Glastonbury's parameters. Now that you're pouring French national power toward the Durandal, I'm sure you fully intend to use and discard me."

Creak-creak-crack-crack resounded an abnormal noise.

It was the sound of Misha, fallen in the distance, pulling its wings of ice out of the ground.

The woman in the red dress held out the tip of her flashing sword and made her defiant announcement.

"Come at me, monster. It's time to teach you that same archangelic power rests condensed in *my* hand, too."

2

Carissa, second princess of Britain.

The Femme Fatale, holy woman of France.

The action they took was a simple one.

They charged directly for Misha Kreutzev.

B-b-b-b-boom!!!!!! The burst exploded after their movement had already taken place. The identity of the loud reverberation, similar to an artillery blast, was a shock wave due to breaking the sound barrier. Carissa and the Femme Fatale, fanned out to either side of the archangel, both aimed for Misha Kreutzev's neck like a huge pair of scissors.

Everyone's eyes opened wide.

Their two swords each sunk into Misha's icy wings.

But even that only lasted a moment.

The blades shaved off the countless wings with the effortlessness of mowing grass before attempting to end Misha's life in one fell swoop.

Misha Kreutzev's hands moved. It pointed each of its palms outward, as though holding open a train door.

That was all.

The Curtana and the Durandal, which had sliced through one death-inducing ice wing after the next, couldn't even deal a grazing blow to the archangel's palms. The swords' motions were gently halted, as though adhering to them.

The angel's head shifted smoothly, setting its hollow eyes on Carissa.

A moment later:

Roar!! A thunderous booming echoed.

It was the sound of Carissa and the Femme Fatale having their respective swords' energies explode. The two were thrown out to the left and right in a large arc. They didn't fall to the ground, but their soles slid over the snow, and the sting of impact remained.

"hboirgPRIORnbugbITIZEvoraghv"

Misha Kreutzev spoke, its head tilting slightly with a *pop.*

Its body turned to face Carissa again.

"nriosgnPRIORITIZEiorseog"

The archangel's palm was thrust out.

And then:

Krshhh!!!!!! Something grazed Carissa's cheek and instantly exploded behind her, shattering an entire hill.

Her reactions couldn't keep up.

She could do nothing but realize that fact as Misha slightly adjusted its palm.

It had corrected the trajectory.

"…!! Out of the way, barbarian!!"

Just before it fired, the Femme Fatale moved faster than the speed

of sound. Traveling in an arc around the supernatural being, she came in at Carissa's side and delivered a flying kick. A normal person might have blown up in that situation, but for them, even something this insane was an act of kindness.

A moment later, something fired from the archangel's palm.

Clumps of snow and dirt exploded spectacularly, but they both still had all their limbs attached.

"What was that? I couldn't even see it."

"Gabriel is a messenger angel. She probably excels in the sending and receiving of information. She uses the information of intuition and indication as a clever decoy, then sends it out in any direction, at any distance, and with any timing. Rely on your normal senses. If you trust your sixth sense, your timing will be off."

"hbwioraEFFECnbsitbgTIVEoargwerge"

"This isn't good. She's gotten a taste, and now she wants more, so."

"No, you just fell for her schemes, you barbarian."

Shwahhh!! Many wings unfolded from Misha's back. They all seemed off. They'd probably been changed so that the speed at which one read indications from the wings would be faster or slower, just like whatever it was that had fired from her palm before.

They couldn't get ahead of them.

If they tried to predict them, it would backfire.

Right after they made sure they knew that, Misha's wings moved.

With speed surpassing sound, over a hundred wings assaulted them at once.

"…!!"

Ba-ga-ga-ga-ga-ga-za-za-za-za-za-ga-ga-ga-ga-gi-gi-gi-gi!!!!!! Countless sparks flew. It was akin to a situation of repelling every shot from a gatling gun, but when the bullets moved around like living creatures, the difficulty soared higher. Just keeping up with the motions was plenty praiseworthy for humans, but Carissa and the Femme Fatale wore ill expressions.

Since decoys hid within the indications they used to get a read on the wings, they always had a timing lag during their initial movements.

Because of that, while they could intercept, they didn't have room to turn things around.

The battle situation stalled, with them only receiving attacks from Misha one-sidedly, descending into a war of attrition.

The battle stalling was not a good thing.

All it did was show how they hadn't found any way to counterattack.

"Something wrong, barbarian?! Didn't the Curtana eat up as much archangel power as the enemy?!"

"Shit. It seems like it's gobbled down enough of the quantity, but I don't know anything about angels. Seems like I'm losing in technique, not strength. What about you?"

"I can't keep up with the power—just with the relic embedded in the hilt! And our objective wasn't to kill an archangel; that would be a pipe dream!!"

Skree!! went the sound of something scraping.

On its face, only recognizable from indentations, the piece corresponding to its mouth squirmed around.

"bzsoINCRgzEASINGeuipghSPEEDerug"

"This...thing...!! We still haven't seen the most of i—!!"

Carissa's face drew back, but Misha surmounted her expectations further.

Over one hundred wings of ice, big and small.

It took them...

...and suddenly aimed not at Carissa or the Femme Fatale—but at the forces of Academy City and Russia.

Damn this thing...!!

A moment later, as the second princess was moving at a supersonic speed, she twisted her body to change direction, diving between the archangel and the soldiers.

To protect the lives of the people from this angelic tyranny.

Misha Kreutzev showed no mercy.

For the archangel had been expecting this opening.

I see.

In that instant, Carissa, time passing unnaturally slowly for her, realized, *Military actions utilizing the martial strength of an archangel. It really goes to show you how worthless my revolution that I forced upon the people was.*

A hundred wings swung down at once.

Someone let out a shout.

And then.

Brrm-brrrrrrrrrrmmmmmmmmmm!!!!!! A massive quaking struck the Russian lands.

Carissa had gritted her teeth, but sticky, fresh blood spurted from between her lips.

Her entire spine groaned in agony.

She'd stopped the attack using the Curtana's power, but caught between the pressure from above and the earth below, she'd very nearly spit out her organs like a full can of soda getting crushed.

But that wasn't even the most terrifying part.

Blood fell from the second princess's palm.

The fragment of the Curtana itself, which had created that sword of flashing light, had shattered, unable to withstand the immense force.

"bndoEFFECTIVENESSlgCONFIRMEDbsdog"

Misha Kreutzev calmly observed her.

And then:

"bguzsegbCONTrlgINUINGvbATTACKrgb"

Vwah!! The hundred wings attacked once again.

As if to say that it planned to repeat any effective attack as many times as it needed.

But Carissa had already lost the sword of flashing light in her hand.

She didn't have the Curtana fragment, either, that had created it.

It came at her.

An attack of absolute wings that would destroy all things.

And this time.

Even sound itself went away.

Everything was frozen.

The French faction, starting with the Femme Fatale; the British faction, represented by the Knight Leader; and the Academy City and Russian forces, who didn't even have a proper recognition of the thing called sorcery. With what just happened before their eyes, they all had stopped in their tracks.

However.

It wasn't because of the destructive force Misha Kreutzev had unleashed.

"...Sure, my sword borrowed the power of all of Britain by routing it through a fragment of the Curtana Second. And it would make sense that it would lose its power once destroyed."

They heard a voice.

It came from the one in the red dress.

From the princess of the queen's nation.

From the woman with mastery over military affairs.

"But I never said I only had *one* Curtana Second fragment, so."

Kzzt!! Flashing pure-white light burst forth.

And not only one.

One in each hand. And then, as if to adorn her dress skirt, ten more swords floated behind her waist.

"...I'm still a princess with her nation on the line, so. Did you think I'd bite the dust that easily?"

"hdtrnDAMAbGEgurgCONFIRMEDhtr"

Skreeeek!! With a shrill noise, Misha repositioned its icy wings.

"bauoCONTINgrlnUINGjjATTACKyhBASEDfvgASSUtgsea-gREDtrrhgsDESTRUCTIONr"

Carissa snorted.

Even as her legs trembled from the effects of sustaining severe injuries, her grin never wavered.

She spoke to the Femme Fatale, who had landed next to her in a single leap.

"...How much longer until our true goal is complete, do you think?"

Preparations for withdrawal were progressing.

Academy City and Russian military alike—currently they were being made to swiftly retreat as directed by the forces of Britain and France. Soldiers were being dragged from broken powered suits, and the wounded were being loaded onto still-operational tanks.

"It depends on how far they need to run before they're safe. If not even the other side of the world will help, then it's over anyway."

"How laid-back of you."

"Do I seem that way?"

The archangel and the two women clashed once more.

Neither Carissa nor the Femme Fatale, each wielding their blades, was unharmed. Misha's ice wings were already moving at incredibly high speeds—and their timing was off thanks to the feints. They'd avoided taking lethal damage, but smaller cuts and scrapes were beginning to accumulate on their bodies. The wounds weren't from direct hits from the ice wings, but rather from the icy shards that broke off when their weapons clashed.

Even so, it didn't change the fact that they were being whittled down.

If this kept up, Carissa and the Femme Fatale would surely exhaust themselves, decisively dulling their movements, and end up taking a mortal blow.

But still.

Neither had confronted the archangel because they wanted to commit suicide.

So swinging her flashing blades in wide, sweeping arcs, Carissa, along with the Femme Fatale, created distance for now.

"Anyway," said Carissa, taking a small communicator from her dress's chest. "I *would* like to keep my life intact. I think it's time I used the next best plan."

"…Would you please not take things out of there? As another woman, I find it quite improper."

Carissa ignored her and spoke into the radio.

"All Pellet Crossbow vehicles on standby. Fire your SAMs at once."

About five kilometers away from the battlefield, behind a hill, was a group of over thirty parked vehicles: some for firing missiles, others for providing targeting assistance via radar, some trucks loaded with additional ammunition, and still others with cranes for loading it all.

The main vehicles were irregularly shaped, like trucks with caterpillar treads. And instead of truck beds, they had beehive-like missile-launching containers on them, each comprising twenty cylindrical tubes.

And nobody said to conserve their ammo.

Starting with one vehicle, twenty flames spurted out in rapid succession. Missiles also fired simultaneously from the other vehicles lined up next to it. The white, stringy smoke began to fill the skies. Over a hundred missiles tore through the heavens.

At first, Misha Kreutzev didn't even bother looking.

It must have decided it could let them all hit it without a problem.

But immediately after, it realized the truth of the matter.

Those projectiles were surface-to-air missiles. In other words, they weren't aiming for Misha, who was on the surface—they were aiming for the Star of Bethlehem, floating high in the sky.

"I don't know if you understand human words, but I'll ask this anyway."

As Carissa swung her flashing swords, she mustered the most wicked smile she could.

"You sure you should be wasting time here? I'd think defending your base has a pretty high priority itself."

"buigbsuiezgsLOSEutrsethtsrth"

"Don't get mad at me."

The second princess casually brushed off even the bloodlust pouring toward her.

"I'm only doing what you did before."

Bchhheeee!! came the explosions.

Carissa and the Femme Fatale were repelled backward simultaneously.

They didn't have time to reestablish themselves.

Misha Kreutzev looked directly upward before using its wings of ice to take immediate flight into the air with the force of a rocket—to intercept the cluster of SAMs aimed at the Star of Bethlehem.

As the Femme Fatale lowered the Durandal, she looked up into the sky. "…I doubt that's enough to bring the fortress down."

"Twisted, distorted, or whatever, angels are angels. They're just slaves that determine requirements programmatically, controlled by a superior's instructions. If the mastermind is trying to do some sort of ritual in that temple up there, it's perfectly easy to predict he would have put together a list of commands so it won't fail."

After Carissa spoke, her body swayed.

…I must have taken more damage than I thought.

She'd just fought an irregular enemy, after all: an archangel. And continuing to draw out power using only the Curtana fragment was a strain in the first place.

Still, that didn't mean she had to retreat now.

The militaristic second princess knew well that war wasn't so simple.

"The SAMs are national resources, too. We can't fire them endlessly, so. Now's our chance to evacuate the wounded. That *target* won't keep tying it down forever."

Even as Carissa commanded her subordinates to "just keep firing," she thought, *Damned monster.*

She spat out the blood in her mouth.

The flashing sword in the second princess's right hand still had immense power within, enough to properly command a nation.

But it was a power for man, created by man.

A true archangel would be one dimension higher than that.

Fact of the matter is: We're up the creek. Couldn't even find a clue as to how humans can beat this thing.

3

The intermittent rumbling continued.

The shaking was strong enough to cause aftershocks even on the Star of Bethlehem floating in the heavens. Kamijou was too afraid to even imagine what was going on down on the ground.

"…We're going higher up," murmured Kamijou while running down a stone-built passage, glancing toward the evenly spaced windows.

With nothing but sky outside, it was hard to tell how high they were. Still, the clouds' height was fixed, and seeing them falling away hinted that the Star of Bethlehem was ascending.

"Answer one. The Star of Bethlehem was originally a heavenly body that a prophet witnessed. By this star's light, the prophet became confident of the Son of God's birth."

"A star floating from artificial methods, huh? That's got a really ominous sound to it. We'll just have to pray we don't go all the way to satellite orbit and that we don't help cause another ice age like a giant meteorite."

Even as they spoke, the passage was creaking and cracking, changing form. But the temporary explosive expansion was gone. It was like a newborn star had cooled and stabilized.

Its size was about forty kilometers in radius.

The spot Kamijou had been in at first was, on the whole, close to the back. The ritual site Sasha told him about, though, was on the edge of the right part, which was longer than the others. As long as Fiamma wasn't after a different destination, he'd be near to it. To stop the archangel Misha rampaging even now, it seemed they'd have to head for the ritual site where Fiamma probably was, but some random high school kid wouldn't be able to run the entire distance on foot.

...But Sasha had escaped from the ritual site at the rightmost part and gotten all the way to where I was.

It would be one thing if she had incredible running abilities, but otherwise, that meant some other method had been prepared for traveling through the Star of Bethlehem at a high speed.

"Answer two. Personally, the option of returning to where I came from after managing to distance myself from it doesn't seem very beneficial."

"Then you can wait here if you want, Sasha."

"Answer three. If I could, I wouldn't be in this trouble."

"I guess not...No way to escape this place without finding a parachute or something. I'll have to really think about that once I beat that asshole's face in."

As he spoke, Kamijou continued through the expansive fortress, guided by Sasha.

"This fortress goes on for miles. It's practically a full marathon. We'll run out of steam just running around, won't we?"

"Answer four. I don't have that much confidence in my stamina, either. I have a method of transportation here."

Eventually, they found it: a monorail. Only one—maybe it really was just for getting around. It looked more like a relative of a car than a train.

And naturally, it wasn't magical.

As Kamijou gaped, Sasha tilted her head. "Question one. Aren't you getting on?"

"Yeah, sure. It's just...The place is like a big rolled-up ball of historical ruins. Why would there be a monorail here?"

"Answer five. Please don't ask me."

Now that he thought about it, there were furnishings that looked historical and footholds and scaffolding used for construction strung along inside Fiamma's base, too. Had he put it together specifically for this sort of design?

...Lesser said there are over two hundred Russian sorcerers. Did they need to repair the existing infrastructure, too, in order to make the place more efficient?

Kamijou and Sasha boarded the monorail.

He didn't know how to control it or anything, but apparently neither did Sasha. It seemed like they only needed to enter a destination, and then the machine would move on its own. Maybe it was more like an elevator than anything else.

For a while, the monorail trailed through the fortress, but eventually it left the proverbial tunnel and came out in the middle of the sky. It looked like they were going on a rail running underneath the fortress.

A view of the sky.

And that sky was dark, without any stars, painted completely over in black.

"The Star of Bethlehem...," murmured Sasha, staring at the purposely constructed darkness. "Opinion one...The star announced Jesus's birth. Is the one known as Fiamma trying to re-create that using only man-made objects?"

The clouds below were dense, but gaps existed in places. Through them, he noticed flashes of red light. That was no nighttime scenery; it was probably flames. He recalled the time when he'd been watching a TV program and they were showing a satellite view of the Amazon. The regions that were doing slash-and-burn farming had glowed red then.

Krrk...Kamijou softly clenched his teeth.

And then it happened. From near the red glow on the earth's surface spurted some kind of water vapor–like stuff. The clouds passed over it a moment later, taking it out of sight, but then suddenly that thick cloud was torn apart. From inside, a dully shining cylindrical object flew out.

"A surface-to-air missile...?!"

And not just one or two, either. Fifty, even a hundred flames blew a wind hole in the night's darkness.

Whoever fired the missiles might have meant them as a last-ditch effort, but some of them were headed straight for the part of the fortress's underside that the monorail car carrying Kamijou and Sasha was traveling along. If they kept going, they'd land a direct hit. And even if the missiles didn't hit the vehicle, as long as they destroyed the rail, there was a good chance Kamijou and Sasha might fall along with it.

But at this point, they had no way to avoid it.

There was nowhere to run in the cramped, boxy monorail car.

An explosion went off.

The monorail car's glass all shattered at once. Fierce winds blew inside. Kamijou tried to cover his ears and curl up, but then he noticed something.

The missiles hadn't hit them directly.

If they had, the monorail car would have been a crushed empty can right now. He and Sasha would have died instantly, too.

The missiles had been shot down—by something.

Kamijou looked.

And then, on the inside of the below-freezing car, he caught his breath.

It had been the archangel Misha Kreutzev.

The huge-winged monster was flying alongside the monorail car, matching its speed.

Kamijou stopped caring about the missiles, exploding one after another, and even the sound of them exploding.

That was the level of tension that ran through him then.

And in the meantime, the archangel flapped its wings again and again, intercepting every one of the countless missiles created with the latest technologies.

"..."

When he got another close-up look, he was surprised by how imposing it appeared.

From afar, it only looked like a human-shaped silhouette with huge wings growing on it, but when he saw it like this, he noticed the similarities to Sasha. Its height, to begin with, was almost six feet. According to Kanzaki, Gabriel was a female angel, but its face was actually smooth, expressionless. It was almost like a doll face still in the manufacturing process. The insufficient hills and valleys actually engendered a strange sort of allure.

It was feminine, surely, but it was more *feminine* than *female*, assumedly to grant it a sense of uncanniness.

Its skin and clothing weren't demarcated, with the silky white cloth showing its body lines. Golden pins fastened the cloth in various places. Its general color scheme was white and gold, but the pale-blue light emanating from its body changed its impression to something viewed on a screen.

The white cloth extended back where the hair would be, spread out in the shape of a trumpet. It looked like a lily, but it probably had some sort of religious meaning.

In a place that wouldn't get in the way of that hair, a small ring made of water was floating. Its speed of rotation would increase or reduce according to the angel's movements as though some sort of rules were at play.

What did Sasha, a genuine Crossist follower, see when she looked at that angel?

Kamijou didn't have the time to ask.

His eyes locked with the archangel's.

Even though its face comprised only indentations, with nothing anyone could call eyeballs, Kamijou definitely felt a terrible sensation in his spine.

Misha Kreutzev made a gesture like someone tilting their head slightly in confusion.

A moment later.

The giant wings on its back filled with power, like someone pulling back on a bow. The movement was clearly trying to attack their monorail car.

...*Shit...?!*

Fiamma of the Right had said that his right arm and Sasha's body were essential to his plans.

However.

Maybe those circumstances didn't matter to Misha Kreutzev.

Its face, expressed only with unevenness, seemed to be watching Kamijou's right hand closely.

The right hand that could cancel out any strange power.

Then, as though drawn to what one could call "her" natural enemy, Misha Kreutzev flapped its wings.

Grrkk-eeeee!! A tremendous sound like two crags ramming together rang out.

For an instant.

Kamijou thought the shock would make his heart would stop—but that didn't actually happen.

That was not the sound of Misha Kreutzev firing an attack at Kamijou and Sasha.

In fact, it was just the opposite.

Someone had intervened, driving an extremely fast flying kick into Misha Kreutzev, knocking it away.

"Question...two. What on earth...?!" said Sasha, groaning.

Nothing normal could have dealt an effective blow against an *archangel*. And they were high in the air—up above fifteen thousand feet. Coming up here by itself had to be impossible for a normal sorcerer.

But Kamijou knew.

He knew exactly one being, one who could overwhelm even saints, one who could probably compete with the magical angel Misha Kreutzev.

A being created by science.

An aggregate of AIM dispersion fields.

And she had dozens of wings coming out of her back, flinging purple lightning every which way.

"Hyouka...Kazakiri...!!"

Kamijou shouted her name as the raging winds gusted past them.

What the heck is she doing here...?!

He doubted she could have heard him.

But she did, just once, glance his way.

For just a moment, a trace of her usual timid nature crept into her face.

A second later, after turning back to face Misha, Kazakiri possessed a fighting spirit he'd never seen in her before.

September 30. Kazakiri, in her angelic winged state, had been under the control of a third party. But he didn't sense that sort of dangerous light from her gaze. Their births may have been different, their body structures may have been different, but a human light filled her eyes. Her hair had changed to a golden hue, and there was a ring over her head and wings on her back, but she was, without a doubt, the Hyouka Kazakiri that Kamijou knew.

They intersected for the blink of an eye.

Since the glasses-wearing girl had stopped in place in order to hold off Misha's follow-up attack, the monorail car zoomed away.

The mouth of a tunnel—another entrance into the fortress—was closing in.

But right before they shot inside, he saw the knocked-away Misha Kreutzev arcing toward Kazakiri. And he saw a strange sword extend from Kazakiri's right hand in response, one that looked like a transformed sinister wing.

He didn't know what became of them.

Because a moment later, the monorail car entered the dark tunnel. And then.

Vr-vvrrrrmmmmm!! A massive shaking hit them after another instant. If they hadn't been in the tunnel, its aftermath alone might have sent the car flying from the rail.

"Damn it!!"

Kamijou ran to the back of the car, but he still couldn't tell from here what was happening in the skies.

…What was that? What the hell happened?!

Judging by the second shock wave that came rushing through, and then the third, their battle hadn't finished.

Kazakiri was supported by Academy City's AIM dispersion fields— How was she here? And why was the fainthearted girl fighting? Kamijou didn't understand anything.

In any case, there was only one thing to do.

This wasn't just for Index anymore. To protect her friend as well, he had to stop Misha Kreutzev's movements as soon as possible.

4

Hyouka Kazakiri.

The girl had abnormally large wings coming from her back, but this was the first time she'd actually flown in the sky. In fact, she hadn't even known whether these wings *had* such a commonplace function. But they weren't giving her any problems. It wasn't that she'd "remembered" how to use them or that she'd learned it anew. It was as though the countless lightning-scattering wings were being remade to bring out the effects she desired—giving her buoyancy just as she wanted.

She'd protect her friends.

That was the feeling with which she'd come all this way, but then she'd found something. A being much like her. And one trying to kill the one on the monorail car, the one she owed her life to.

In the skies, over fifteen thousand feet in the air, she glared at the enemy before her.

They resembled each other.

They weren't humanlike, but they still looked feminine. Giant wings sprouted from their backs. A small halo hovered above their heads. They possessed immense strength, which carried the risk of collateral damage. In other words, their existences were supported by a kind of power.

As they faced off, and as she thought about how they were alike, she realized something.

I see.
Almost like an angel.

*　　*　　*

Was that her impression of the enemy before her or an impression of herself? Hyouka Kazakiri didn't strictly make a distinction. She didn't need to. Any impressions she had of *her* applied to herself as well—as all impressions she had of herself applied to *her*. She had the vague notion that's just how they were.

What was the other one thinking and feeling?

Did she have the ability to think and feel at all?

Did that apply to herself, too?

Was she herself truly succeeding at thinking and feeling from her heart?

In this situation, where starting to consider it too deeply seemed like it would lock her into an endless loop, the two monsters, paused in midair, eventually began to slowly move.

Hyouka Kazakiri tightened her grip on the "sword" made of the same essence as her wings.

In contrast, the angel of water gently waved its empty right hand and produced an icy blade from midair.

They didn't need a signal.

By the time one had moved, the other had already begun as well.

That was their connection as they clashed head-to-head.

Boom!!

A spherical shock wave fired out and spread—endlessly.

The air tingled and shook.

The shock wave had the density of a physical wall, and it even rattled the floating stone fortress. Several rooms caved in, but their fragments, instead of raining down on the surface, hung suspended as though liquid in a zero-gravity space, before being reabsorbed into the fortress.

There was no time to idly watch.

Even as that happened, the battle continued.

As the monsters' swords locked together, the giant wings on their backs wriggled like living creatures.

They howled.

And then they crashed into each other.

Ba-bang!! Ba-ga-zk-zk-gak-gak-gak-greeee!! With momentum exceeding the speed of sound, dozens of blades attacked their targets, each at its own angle. But victory was not decided. The reason was that as both of them continued their fierce offensive, they kept enough power in store to deal with the other's.

Icy wings swung, icy wings tore apart; lightning wings attacked, lightning wings broke. The fragments, severed from their masters, turned into fine particles in midair and scattered, becoming an all-encompassing snowstorm of lights that took on color. They looked like small feathers, left behind in the wake of a white bird soaring away.

Still flapping its innumerable wings, the angel of water also swung the watery sword in its hand horizontally in an attempt to decapitate Kazakiri. Kazakiri repelled the assault with her own sword before preparing for a new attack.

The face of the angel so close to her was blank.

It was like an incomplete doll, and while its face possessed alluring irregularity, it didn't have any isolated parts, like eyes, a nose, or a mouth. It looked like a smooth mask—and the valley corresponding to its mouth was writhing.

It sounded like quiet mutterings.

The words didn't belong to any nation. Maybe it was in a range unperceivable by human ears.

But Kazakiri could hear. She could understand. She could feel.

She couldn't comprehend every little thing perfectly, of course. She probably couldn't tell it to speak her language, either. But she could manage to pick out words in the sentences here and there.

"hbo…RETURN…fbyuo…"

At first, it was the color of an emotion.

When she realized what the color was, the words creating that color, too, began rising to the surface.

"RETURN. frPOSITION. CORRECT. SEAT. uj. HEAVENLY PLANE. ORIGINAL. MUST BE. gePLACE."

Something was blurred.

The contours of the angel of water, whom she'd thought was a single being, swayed slightly.

It wasn't that something was overlapping it. Nor was something trying to burst out. Kazakiri didn't possess a body made of physical matter—and that was how she penetrated its identity.

"...Someone is forcing in power of a different format...?"

She could see fire.

Its presence was like oil to water.

The two kinds of energy had been poured into a cup and stirred up, creating what must have once been a properly blended angel. However, as time passed, they separated, and the two energies were now trying to create a line of demarcation in the single container.

Two powers must not be placed into one container.

One could have called that purity the polar opposite of Kazakiri, who was an aggregate of every single AIM dispersion field. They seemed the same at first, but in reality, they were based on two entirely different things. Two who could have been alike precisely because they stood at opposite ends. Perhaps that was the relationship between Kazakiri and the angel.

Did that amount to blasphemy, for her?

A color of anger was in the angel as it formed words.

"go back. necessary. workt. conduct. fiamma. advantage. interest. alignment. yplan. cooperate"

"...If that is the reason you would harm my precious friends, then I'll use all the power I can muster to stop you."

"damage. ignore. prioritize. return. correct. position. necessary. obstruction. evil. synonymy. decision. everything"

Zzzaa!! An enormous vortex of energy began to roil about from inside the angel of water.

Its watery sword swung in an even wider arc, colliding with Kazakiri's feather sword, and both gained a small amount of distance.

The angel of water raised its sword overhead.

And then it happened: The angel of water's halo gave a slight jerk. Its focus diverted away from Kazakiri to something else.

"capture"

Its mouth opened.

The mouth of the archangel who could now see naught but its own objective.

"necessary. information. parchment. acquire"

5

Still carrying Last Order, Accelerator climbed into a civilian car parked in the snow. He was in the passenger seat, with Misaka Worst in the driver's.

"Where to, sir?"

"Sneaking around in the shadows is just gonna wear me out. Quickest way to make things right is to jump right into the middle of the chaos."

"Understood," said Misaka Worst in an offhand tone, inserting the key given to her by Elizalina and starting the engine. She didn't seem to have any difficulty driving with one hand, maybe because the car was an automatic.

The headlights' glow danced, piercing across the unnatural darkness that had fallen. The passenger car, driven by Misaka Worst, made it out of the small town quickly, coming out onto the snowfield.

"About five minutes until the border...Man, you can tell all the way from here how insane the battle is. *Unscientific* would be an understatement."

A giant fortress had risen in the dark skies.

It was incredibly huge. It had to be quite a distance away, but it was practically covering an entire swath of the sky as though a cumulonimbus cloud had come overhead.

And then, with that fortress behind them, two faintly glowing angels clashed again and again in midair. Their respective wings tangled together and plucked the others' out, and shock wave-like shouts were sent scattering into their surroundings. As their battle continued, a starry sky, equally as unnatural as the blackened night, began to spread.

"Gah...ah...?!"

It was just like whenever he was near Unabara. But this time, the pressure crushing Accelerator's chest in the passenger's seat was extraordinary, nothing like those times. He felt like it would be strange if nothing happened to his heart. Something about that starry sky wasn't right.

Groaning through the pressure in his chest, Accelerator said, "...You really have no clue what that is? If you're designed to pick up anger and hatred from the Misaka network, then you should be able to draw information from it, too, right?"

"Which angel are you referring to? The one over there with the ice wings? Or that one with the lightning wings?"

"..."

"And for your information, just because Academy City has the information, I don't think that necessarily means it's scientific."

...Which meant maybe it was only natural not to have enough strength with *only* science in order to save Last Order, who was deeply related to *it*.

That thing.

The sky those monsters danced in—that was the world wherein lived the cause of Last Order's suffering.

So maybe, in order to rescue Last Order from there, Accelerator himself would need to ascend into that territory.

How?

Aiwass's power had been overwhelming. Accelerator's black wings alone didn't put up any kind of fight. His trivial villainous crown couldn't protect the little girl. What should he do, then? How could he protect her smile from this unreasonable world?

The sheaf of parchment hidden in his inside pocket almost felt sarcastic in its insistence on its own existence.

The scribble-like spells and magic circles drawn on them were linked to their technology, which could use "mysteries" on the same level as the angel Amata Kihara created on September 30 or even higher levels. He would fight a problem where theory didn't apply in a way that ignored theory. It was a dangerous gamble, one that came with many unknown risks. Normally, he would have needed to strictly avoid entrusting Last Order's fate to something like that. But still, maybe at this point that was his only chance to win. It was like groping through utter darkness, not knowing what paths would lead to a cliff.

And then—

—It happened.

The two monsters fighting in the skies, tangled together, rapidly descended. The scene would have been so powerful to a religious man that it would add a page to the legends; but Accelerator didn't shed tears of emotion. He didn't have time. The monsters with those wings growing out of them were, no matter how one thought about it, headed straight for their car.

More specifically, it looked like one of them was after Accelerator while the other chased it.

"...Did they catch a whiff of this parchment?"

Feeling it in his pocket, Accelerator grinned evilly.

He recalled Elizalina saying something about there being a chance the Russian organization responsible for this situation wouldn't be able to complete their little project without retrieving the parchment.

In the driver's seat, Misaka Worst, gripping the steering wheel, whistled. "Phew!! What now, what now? This could be more dangerous than a hurricane rushing our way!!"

"Natural disasters and man-made ones have a simple difference," said Accelerator in a low voice, opening the passenger's seat window. Without paying attention to the fiercely cold, stabbing winds, he said, "It's whether there's an enemy to kill. How nice it is to have a clear target in front of me. Means I don't have to let anything annoying hold me back, like my anger not having an outlet."

After finishing, he leaned his upper body out from the passenger's seat. Then he sat on the window frame like some motorcycle gang member in the old days.

"You take care of the kid. Buy me some time until I can settle the score."

"Not sure about you trusting Misaka. She's absolutely awful with that stuff, you know."

"You're lucky you're useful. You still have a chance not to get killed even after a shitty joke like that."

"Mm-hmm. Misaka likes that better."

He didn't have any more time to chat. The two monsters would make landfall in a moment.

Accelerator flipped his electrode's switch.

Manipulating air currents to extend four tornado-like wings from his back, he threw himself from the car window frame.

He didn't crash into the ground.

His body shot through the battlefield like a rocket.

Another monster had just joined the fight.

6

Like the advent of a solar eclipse, darkness had spread. In addition, a large number of unnatural points of light twinkled like the interior of a poorly constructed planetarium. A few, however, were straightforwardly joyful at the sight, which one could express as either eerie or mystical. Even now, all kinds of explosions and rumblings echoed in the distance.

Amid all that, Grickin was walking through a snowy forest.

He was the Russian soldier who had operated the mobile anti-air gun with Hamazura and Digurv to protect the settlement that had been under attack from privateers.

Currently, because Academy City's forces had garrisoned there, the danger of a Russian follow-up attack had decreased. Thanks to them building temporary housing, the people of the settlement no longer needed to worry about freezing to death in a blizzard, even with most of its original wooden buildings destroyed.

"..."

However, Grickin couldn't meekly accept the favor.

He'd come from the Russian military. And the air base he belonged to had been attacked by Academy City. Their conduct and the armaments they'd used had been wholly different; those providing emergency supplies to the settlers and those merciless killers seemed clearly to be separate units, one official and one not. Even so, he wasn't in a state where he could simply trust them.

It was different from anger.

At the core of that resistance, there was fear.

...From the moment I fought the privateers, I no longer had a home in Russia. Maybe I should have just gone to Elizalina while I still had the chance.

That was what Grickin was thinking, but getting away from the settlement wasn't why he was walking around the snowy forest like this right now. Even if he was going to the Alliance, he felt an obligation to thank the people of the settlement who had saved him.

Then why was he wandering around a place like this at all?

Where the hell did that kid get off to...?

He was lost.

There were children, too, in the settlement. And once they were freed from their state of extreme tension from the privateer attack, they'd started running around to play again—that was how kids were. Maybe they'd gotten even more excited now that the danger to their lives had passed. After all, even the adults in the settlement had started drinking and carousing.

In that time, a girl of about ten had vanished.

The children she'd been playing with said they hadn't seen where she'd gone, just that she suddenly wasn't there anymore.

An adult like Grickin would have been somewhat cautious of this unnatural night sky (even if he knew he couldn't do anything about it). But the girl who had disappeared was just a child. She was at an age where she still believed in Santa Claus. It was even possible she'd wandered out too far while looking up at the sky with some kind of hope.

But the Russian winters were severe. The biting cold, for one thing—and there was a significant possibility of encountering a carnivorous beast woken from its hibernation by the clamor of bombings and artillery fire. To top it off, he'd heard there were land mines seeded throughout this area. This wasn't an environment you could safely let your child play in.

The girl's mother had apparently wanted to join the search, but everyone else stopped her. The child's life was important, but if she succumbed to the chill or the land mines in a second tragedy, that would defeat the purpose. Instead, a small number of people, starting with Grickin, were now looking around here and there in the settlement.

Their group was small, so only Grickin was here right now.

He'd walked about three kilometers from the settlement, but he hadn't spotted anything even resembling a girl. He wondered if a little kid's legs could even bring them this far in this amount of snow. It might be possible with a child's stamina, if they were walking with the intent to die, but if she'd simply been playing, that would reduce her motivation to come all this way; normally, she'd decide to go back to the settlement. So should he go back for now?

As Grickin began to mull it over, he spotted an indistinct figure moving through the blizzard.

But it was large.

"?!"

He rushed to hide behind the trees, thinking he'd accidentally found a bear or something. But that wasn't it. Wild bears didn't wear white combat clothing made for soldiers operating in extremely cold regions. He could tell from its design that they were Russian army uniforms, but he'd never put his arms through anything that high-class.

...An unofficial saboteur team?! Wait, isn't that the unit everyone calls the Eastern Angels of Death?!

It was a team that mainly relied on sniping or bombings to assassinate important targets from other countries and one that had provoked wars between nations that brought disadvantage to Russia. During the Cold War, people whispered about them like an urban legend: All someone in power had to do was write a name on a piece of paper, and they'd immediately come assassinate them.

This may have been wartime, but they weren't the sort one could run into for no reason. If that team was walking around in those clothes, then they were already dragging tragedy along behind them on chains.

What were they doing here?

And why had they gotten out of their vehicles to advance on foot?

Grickin couldn't help but think of Digurv and the others in the settlement, which had been targeted so Russia could create a frontline base, and the Academy City people who had garrisoned it.

But if Grickin, who had been on indoor service in the air base here, took on a team of handpicked elite agents, he'd have no chance of winning. He could only see one right now, but if they were in the middle of some military operation, they'd have multiple people on the move, even if this was for unofficial combat.

The best thing to do would be leave here immediately and go back to the settlement.

If those Academy City people did something—and it bothered him to say it—they'd handle this team of saboteurs. These guys didn't win through massive numbers; they were pros at secret maneuvers with only a few people, causing enemy military forces to fall into chaos. If one only knew where they were and the timing of their attack, one could repel them with numbers.

Grickin took a step away from the tree he was hidden behind.

But he couldn't take a second.

The figure through the blizzard had suddenly jerked to a stop. *Shit*, Grickin thought, feeling a pressure from a set of eyes.

Nobody else was around—and that was why Grickin clearly sensed those eyes, staring straight toward him.

"…"

He was at quite a distance, but even so, each read the other's silence.

A moment later, the agent put his assault rifle stock to his shoulder, then swung the muzzle mercilessly in Grickin's direction.

"Damn it!!"

Forcing down the terror strangling his heart, Grickin turned his back. The rifle bullet stabbed into the trunk of the tree he'd just been up against. As the gunshot sounded, a piece of tree bark bounced off and grazed his cheek. Without time to reflect on that bit of luck, he simply kept running through the snowy forest.

It didn't seem like he'd have a chance to win.

Simply fleeing the one soldier coming after him wouldn't save him.

He called me in, he thought, desperately working his legs, which seemed like they were about to collapse out of fear. *I don't know how many people they have, but if they surround me, I won't be able to escape!!*

The snow under his feet as he ran was flung about by a rifle bullet. He kept running, practically in a stumble, and then actually twisted his foot and fell into the snow. But he didn't have time to stop. Even now, an enemy aiming for him was following him from behind. The more the distance dropped, the higher the chance that he'd die. But when he forced his snow-covered body up again to start running, he was presented with yet another obstacle.

But not an enemy.

It was the girl who had been lost until now.

She must have come here after hearing the shots ringing out in the snowy forest. For Grickin, that was the worst thing that could have happened. There was no guarantee he'd be able to escape even on his own—if a kid was holding him back, they'd definitely be overtaken.

But that didn't mean he could leave her here.

The agent hadn't confirmed Grickin's identity before discharging his rifle. He was simply getting rid of any witnesses. And it probably didn't matter if that witness was a civilian or a child.

"Shit!!"

Scooping up the confused child, Grickin tried to run farther. But his feet caught in the deep snow, and his body fell into it, his balance ruined by her unexpectedly heavy weight.

The soldier approached.

Grickin could see, even from this distance, the agent's finger pressing the trigger.

Until.

Baaaang!! A gunshot echoed out through the snowy forest.

Grickin had unconsciously closed his eyes, but he felt no pain.

Nervously, he opened his eyes and saw the soldier fallen on the ground a short distance away. A lump of snow piled up on a branch, about twenty pounds' worth, had suddenly fallen on his head.

It was not a natural occurrence, of course; the gunshot just now hadn't been from the assault rifle in the soldier's hands. A third party had fired at the trunk of the tree near him, from somewhere. After all, hitting a big target sitting still was easier than a small target that was constantly moving.

"Are you okay?!"

He heard a shout. Japanese—rare in these parts. Another gunshot went off. The snow on the ground near the agent trying to get up flew about. He saw the brawny soldier raise his hands.

"Grickin, tie him up!! That was a lucky surprise attack that happened to work. If we take him on for real, we won't be able to deal with him!!"

He remembered that voice. He looked toward where it came from just as Shiage Hamazura was running toward him, weaving between the trees, a gun in his hand. In a moment, as though irritated by how Grickin still wasn't moving, he tied the agent's hands behind his back with barbed wire.

"…Why…?" murmured Grickin, not thinking properly, before remembering the situation. He peeled the girl he had been trying to protect off him and said, "Never mind, it doesn't matter. Let's get away from here. The guy you just tied up is from an elite Russian unit. His friends will figure it out soon from the gunshots and radio silence. We have to run before they surround us."

"I've got a bone to pick with them."

"?"

Grickin frowned as a girl approached, following in Hamazura's wake. Her name was Takitsubo, if he remembered correctly. She'd been sick with something until a little while ago, but it seemed like she'd recovered.

Hamazura looked her way, and Takitsubo dutifully took the girl's hand. Then, as natural as anything, she led her away—so she wouldn't hear what they were about to say.

"The Kremlin Report."

"The what?"

"There's a nuclear launch silo near the settlement that isn't active anymore. The top Russian officers think Academy City might seize it, so they want to hit first and deploy a bioweapon in the area. Apparently, they set up a process for handling all this in advance."

"...Bastards...," groaned Grickin.

Normally, such a story would have been immediately unbelievable. But the presence of that unofficial combat unit, the soldier after his life just moments ago, had been far too sinister.

"You mean that unit is gonna spread a horrible virus or something?! Even if we had all the settlers evacuate now, I don't know if they'd have enough time!!"

"Well, Takitsubo was the one who read the report because it was in Russian, but apparently they have to go through certain steps to spray the weapon. There was a report on predicted casualties that had data on wind direction, temperature, humidity, and stuff like that. It seems like the humidity—the amount of moisture in the air—is important for spreading the contagion, but it's highly possible it'll turn into diamond dust with how cold it is."

"In that case..."

"But if they use a large amount of water vapor to change the temperature and humidity, the contagion will spread out like an explosion. They want to take this heat-retaining gel and make it into powder, then scatter it upwind from the target point. Special gel that won't freeze even at these temperatures. Once they've optimized the temperature and humidity in the appropriate area, they can unleash the weapon in question. If a person goes into it one time, the virus will survive by the infected person's body temperature and moisture, creating a carrier."

"Then we might be able to do something if we can just stop them from spreading that heat-retaining gel they need for the first step."

"It said on there it was called the Steam Dispenser. It's a device for making the gel into powder and shooting it into the air. Like a special humidifier, I guess. Anyway, that, uh, unit or whatever. We have to somehow destroy that machine before they take action."

Somehow.

That was easy to say, but it meant fighting that elite unit and winning. If the enemies moved as a group, two people wouldn't be enough to take them out in a surprise attack.

"…What do we do? Call the Academy City forces garrisoned in the settlement?"

"There's no time. And if we do something big, it might make them push up their schedule for spreading the stuff. We can estimate the Steam Dispenser's rough position by geographical and weather data with the wind direction. We haven't figured out exactly where it is. If that unit starts right now, we're already too late. And…"

Hamazura paused.

Grickin lowered his face slightly at his silence. "Sorry…"

"It's fine. But we need to move before the ones left get suspicious. Grickin, can you drive a car? Here's the key. We hid the jeep three hundred meters west of here. You take the girl and go back to the settlement for now."

"But then you'll be—?!"

"More of those guys could be wandering around here, so we can't leave the girl here. It's too dangerous to have her walk back alone, and bringing her to the battlefield is out of the question. Please, escort her back. And the soldier I tied up, too."

After saying that, Hamazura took out his cell phone.

"Let's trade phone numbers. There's nothing around here, but apparently we still get a connection because of some relay antennas. I'll contact you once I find the Steam Dispenser. At that point, even if they realize Academy City's doing something, I can put a stop to them before they start the spread. And then you have to do whatever you can to persuade the Academy City soldiers to have the people in the settlement go on an exodus. If I don't contact you for thirty minutes, same thing. Be careful of the wind direction. It may not matter much if they actually spray the weapon, but it's probably better than moving around without thinking. I'd actually like them to run away right now, but not if they run blindly to where the Steam Dispenser is waiting for them. Understand?"

"..."

"Do you understand me, Grickin?! If something happens to me, and you don't do your job, a lot of people in that settlement could die!!"

"..."

"It's impossible that every single person in the Russian army wants to use a bioweapon like that! That's why they sent in a team that would willingly take on the heartless mission of the first spraying operation!! If they get a certain amount of results here or whatever, those soldiers will lose all self-control!! Meaning the same thing could happen in the rest of Russia!! We have to avoid that. I don't want anyone being a victim—not any of the Academy City soldiers or anyone in the settlement. Do you understand me now, Grickin?!"

"Yeah, I understand you, damn it!! I'll protect those settlers with my life. You'd better not die out there, either!!"

Hamazura and Grickin, after exchanging cell phone numbers, slapped their palms together as if to run the plastic devices into each other. They said nothing more after that. Takitsubo, judging that their conversation was over, returned with the girl. Grickin took the girl's hand, put the tied-up soldier on his shoulder, then headed off for where they'd hidden the jeep.

Hamazura put his cell phone in his pocket, then turned to Takitsubo and said, "We should go, too."

"Hamazura. Considering the weather and geographical data in the report, I suspect the spot is about five hundred meters north of here."

Takitsubo spoke smoothly, perhaps because she'd been in charge of reconnaissance for Item. It didn't have anything to do with her ability, but she'd probably polished the skill to figure out plans based on data, too.

"There's a small mountain, less than a hundred meters tall, and the wind blows down from there toward the nuclear launch silo and the settlement."

"Won't be at the mountaintop. They're on a time limit, too—they want to wrap things up as fast as they can. I think they'll try to quickly set up the Steam Dispenser as close to the foot as they can manage."

Hamazura walked up to the place the soldier had been lying a few moments ago, then picked up the assault rifle and magazine he'd been carrying. Its weight and texture were entirely different from his handgun. He doubted he could use it properly, but going in with a single pistol would be far too unreliable.

For just a moment, the chill of the lethal weapon gave him pause.

But then he looked up to shake off the feeling, slung the band around his shoulder, and took a determined step toward the mountain to the north.

"Hamazura. Let's finish it quickly. I'm sick of this war."

"Yeah. And I gotta say, I hate this solar eclipse. Least they could've done is given us a view of the aurora."

7

As Accelerator blew away the white snow on the ground like a blast wave, he charged at the two angels. For just a moment, he considered which of the two, clashing their blades together, he should launch a preemptive strike on.

Whatever the case was, they were monsters with wings growing from their backs.

He had no responsibility to help, either.

In which case.

Accelerator applied his reflection to purposely intervene between the two angels.

A thunderous *ba-bam!!* rang out.

Of the two angels, his reflection didn't work properly on the one flapping wings of water with a doll-like face. It was just like Vodyanoy and the others at the remains of the air base. He was definitely using his reflection ability, but the watery wings twisted and squished like candy, gouging out a forest nearby, ground and all, and flinging it into the air.

The rebound angle was shallow. If the angel pressed Accelerator any harder, it would hit him directly, too.

But his expression didn't change. The other angel—the one that looked like a woman wearing glasses—his reflection worked on her wings just fine. Ignoring the angel, surprised almost like a human would be, Accelerator forcibly converted his attack vector on the angel wearing the glasses.

He converged it into a single point, then brutally slammed it into the water angel's chest.

All sound disappeared.

Ignoring gravity, the angel's body, which had been freely dancing through the air, shot over three hundred meters backward. The monster fell spectacularly, shooting across the surface while pulling up the ground underneath like an airplane crash.

The reason Accelerator had gone after the water angel first was simple.

His ability worked on one of them—and not on the other. It made sense to go for the more troublesome one first.

"You...are...?"

The angel wearing the glasses, who probably wielded a power of a sort even Accelerator could understand, stammered, sounding baffled.

In Japanese. Without any blurring like with Aiwass.

"You controlled my wings, made of an aggregate of AIM dispersion fields...?"

"I'm surprised a monster like you has a brain in there capable of having a serious Q and A."

Accelerator opened his jacket and showed her the sheaf of parchment he had shoved into his inside pocket.

"Did this thing draw *you* here, too?"

"...?"

The scientific angel frowned, as though confused.

But then—

Whumm!! Something like a wall of pressure spread out over the area. It was like an invisible explosion—and it had a strange, unknowable killing intent. When he looked at ground zero of the immense negative emotions, more than a single human could ever output on their own, the knocked-away water angel was just getting up.

The snow disappeared.

All the white drifts in a five-hundred-square-meter range centered on the angel melted and turned into water.

Zm-zm-zm-zm-zm-zm-zm-zm-zm-zm-zm-zm!!!!!! A huge amount of fluid was absorbed into the water angel. In the blink of an eye, its already enormous wings changed into something even more fiendish.

"How candid. Trying to introduce yourself?"

Accelerator closed his jacket and turned to face his adversary.

While standing side by side with the science angel, as it were.

"Um, I..."

"I'll deal with you later," said Accelerator, sounding bored. "Got no interest in Academy City–made stuff. I'm getting the feeling that other monster has the key I need to save the kid."

He'd learned something from the initial clash: Both angels were monsters but not as strong as Aiwass.

It was obvious when it came to the science angel—his reflection and vector manipulation worked on her. Even with the unknown water angel, though, if he could blow it away using the science angel's power, it was far from being Aiwass.

After all.

Aiwass never even left an opportunity to counterattack.

I can win.

It was a cynical method of judgment—but Accelerator knew it wasn't wrong.

That was when it happened:

"…hbuiesdfosfnisadofhjohnvouazeswhfpiASNFcpiAENFpiAN-Jvpidnkljndsigps…"

The water angel's mouth writhed about.

Something was coming out. A small sound, hard to make out.

He didn't know what country's language that was in the first place, but…

"…sergvSCOPEhySETTING…"

A clear revolution occurred in Accelerator's ears.

He felt like someone had shown him another painting buried inside a trompe l'oeil.

"DROPgrePREPARATION…djkuCOMPLETE"

This language.

Accelerator knew this language.

As he brought up his face in surprise, every one of the watery wing tips pointed up to the ominous night sky. Almost like a radio antenna. Almost like it was receiving a signal from the heavens.

And then.

Its voice, which had just become clear, said:

"Command *Eradication*——dropping."

The night sky sparkled.

He didn't have time to see why.

Tens of millions of destructive stones began to rain down over an area about two kilometers in radius.

Divine punishment, of the same nature as the power even he couldn't fully reflect.

"?!"

He couldn't react in time.

Dodge or block? Before he could think about it, the tempest of destruction slammed into him with all its brutality. He lost his concept of where the sky and the ground was. By the time he realized he'd taken a direct hit, his body had been flung through the air. He tried to alleviate the damage through vector manipulation, but the taste of blood crawled up from the bottom of his throat. Snow, dirt, and everything else whipped up and around, whiting out Accelerator's vision.

"Gh...gah...agh?!"

When he slammed into the ground, his voice was harsh but broken. Breathing felt impossible. Using his ability, he controlled vectors to expel the blood accumulated in his throat all at once, finally regaining the ability to breathe.

You piece of shit...!! What the hell is this...?!

In his vision, now white with the risen snow, he saw one spot of color in front of him.

A blue light.

The symbol of destruction known as an archangel.

"..."

He saw the night sky once again taking on an uncanny glow.

It wasn't over after that one volley. Whether it took five or ten, the water angel would continue to execute this until its target no longer moved.

You can...fuck right off...

Even as his body creaked and groaned, Accelerator slowly stood up.

He couldn't afford to die here.

There was still something he needed to do.

He couldn't afford to lose—not until he tore apart every single bit of the unfairness binding Last Order.

Doesn't matter if I can beat it on paper or not. As long as I have a reason to crush it, that's all I need!

Boom!! went an explosion.

Manipulating the vectors of his leg forces, Accelerator dove straight at the monster's blue light.

And then the water angel delivered more of its heartless words.

"WAVEkoTWO. ATTACKwagrCOMMENCINGwsPREPARATION. THIRTY SECONDiseUNTIL SECONDnvspERADICATION DROP"

Meanwhile.

Bbbrrrrrrrrrmmmm!!!!!! The thunderous boom shook Russia's night sky.

It was the first Eradication.

"She's going too far," murmured Fiamma of the Right from the Star of Bethlehem, floating over seven thousand meters high. The incredible shaking made it even to his feet, but this one hadn't been a surface shock wave that had climbed up here.

It had been collateral.

The magic circle for Eradication that the archangel had prepared had deployed even higher in the sky than the Star of Bethlehem. And when Gabriel had restrictively dropped that Eradication, it had shaved off part of the Star of Bethlehem floating directly underneath.

Just by looking at the color in the night sky, he estimated she would fire a second volley within thirty seconds. The damage to the Star of Bethlehem would surely grow.

But there was no major change in Fiamma's expression.

He only had to let her do as she pleased. In any case, now that the Star of Bethlehem had expanded enough, it had acquired self-repairing abilities. Even now, part of the crushed castle floated in midair, trying to return to its initial placement.

Fiamma, who had linked his senses to an extent with Gabriel, who he himself controlled, said "Is this all?" in a bored-sounding tone.

"Is this all my enemies amount to? I *know* you could simulate how the war would change if an archangel appeared."

The angel that seemed to belong to Academy City had whet his interest ever so slightly but hadn't affected him much. And a certain esper, positioning to battle alongside that Academy City angel. He was probably the treasure, so to speak, of the science side—but even together, they couldn't take down Misha Kreutzev.

The effects of Eradication were tremendous.

Even now, the Academy City monsters were persisting in their attack on Misha. But they couldn't deny the damage was building up. At this rate, a second and third wave of Eradication in quick succession would stop them in their tracks for sure. After all, they couldn't avoid it or defend against it.

No need to decide things in a single attack.

If Gabriel could slowly but surely whittle away at their strength, she could annihilate them with that accumulated damage.

This was the brute force of numbers the Roman Church so excelled in.

It was the same as river water eroding the land.

"If this is how it will end…"

Fiamma's fingers brushed his staff.

"If nobody will stop me…"

That Soul Arm he had applied to the archangel's control, embedded with the remote-control Soul Arm for Index.

"…then my Eradication *will* cover the world."

That was when it happened.

Suddenly, a voice spread from within Fiamma of the Right, separate from his sense of hearing.

He knew exactly who owned that "voice."

"…It's been so long, Acqua. Do you still intend to call yourself a member of God's Right Seat? Or have you reverted to the simple mercenary's life by now?"

"It matters not, so long as I am in a position to stop your atrocities."

"And how will you do that?" murmured Fiamma of the Right in a casual tone, twirling his staff. "Six billion now cross blades in heated battle throughout the world. You are but one man among them in this situation. How will you save them all?"

"..."

"In fact, *you* are the symbol of those battles. An affirmation of good, clothed in violence. You were a wonderful pawn, destroying unknown threats throughout the lands and sowing your seeds to the people you saved. People look up to you, thanks to that. And to your way of resolving problems through violence."

And I have no use for a pawn whose role has ended.

Even regret toward releasing that great martial power was not present in Fiamma's voice.

"I'm quite sure you understand why this war broke out. It was I who pulled the trigger. But bullets cannot fire without gunpowder. I know you comprehend the meaning behind this structure—and I will still ask you. How *will* you save everyone?"

"And that is enough reason to wield an archangel against the people?"

"Will you stop me? It would be resolution by violence, once again. A story unfit even for a farce—but how would you do it? Even if you join that Academy City angel, victory is already decided. You must know this—you *are* the one who infiltrated that city to retrieve Vento on September 30."

A scornful voice.

"The existence of Academy City's angel distorts the planes and produces a strong negative effect on sorcery control. That was what forced Vento into a needlessly agonizing battle. You are unable to fight on its side. And if you use martial force anyway, the most you would do is cause mutual competition, mutual chaos."

"..."

"And if you took turns battling individually, Misha Kreutzev's raw power would outstrip you all. Despite how it may look, it *is* a true archangel. The only one who could possibly win in a fair fight is *me*."

Thus, he spoke his ultimatum: an utterly one-sided conclusion.

"You have *some* power, certainly, but only as a piece on *my* game board. However you choose to wield your sword now, however you utilize your violent force, the archangel will not be stopped. I can yield you the right to at least put up a futile resistance, but the better idea would be to twiddle your thumbs and watch."

"*I see.*"

And then Fiamma heard a chuckle.

Acqua had laughed at him.

"*Then I will show you a way using no 'violent force,' as you say.*"

Boom!!!!!!

A moment later, a third of Misha Kreutzev's total power was gone.

An angel was a body comprising a certain type of energy. It didn't normally possess a physical form. The insides, for lack of a better term, of Misha Kreutzev's nonphysical body had suddenly and drastically thinned. And that was enough to make Fiamma, his senses partially linked to her, catch his breath.

"What…did you do? No, this is…"

"*Have you forgotten? I am Acqua of the Back. One of God's Right Seat, the most secret organization in the Roman Church. The symbol of blue, the moon, and the back—and the one who commands Gabriel of the Four Archangels.*"

"Wait, have you…taken it into your own body…?!"

"*The sealing and release of telesma—angelic power—is the most basic fundamental in Crossist spellcasting. And my body itself functions as the greatest medium to link with Gabriel…If I thoroughly absorb this water-aspected telesma, it goes without saying what will happen to its source, which is Gabriel's power.*"

"…"

It was *insane*.

No normal sorcerer, to start with, would ever consider packing all the power of an archangel into their own single body. No matter how one viewed it, the person would explode and die in the process.

However…

"It is certainly not impossible."

Acqua's voice cut through the walls of common sense.

"In fact, you set your eyes on that Russian nun you used because she was able to do just that."

"You fool…It was only because she had the knowledge and capacity that it flowed naturally into her during Angel Fall!! It's not something just anyone can do. Even if you cloned Sasha Kreutzev herself, I doubt the clone would have the same capacity!! Without that much inborn talent, even I would never consider using it in that manner!!"

"That is not what I am saying…If someone else can do it, then so can I. I offer only that simple fact."

I see, thought Fiamma. *He is still part of God's Right Seat. I suppose this means trying to argue with him using common sense is the wrong move.*

"Then go ahead and try."

"You can be certain that I will."

"Still, I do hope you're aware that your reckless challenge *will* shatter your power. What you're doing is suicide, plain and simple."

One man stood alone in snowy Russia.

He was a short distance from the national border with the Independent Nations. He was distant from Fiamma's fortress, but that presented no inconvenience for the spell he was about to perform.

He'd stuck his great sword, far longer than his height, into the ground halfway and used it to support his own tall frame.

The surrounding air distorted.

The man stood in the middle of an abnormal swaying, as if a large amount of sugar had been dissolved into water.

Immense power.

It flowed inside.

Attached with the color blue and responding to the light of the moon—an enormous amount of telesma.

"Whoooooooooooooooooooooooooooooooooooooooooooooooooo ooooooooooooooooooooooooooooooooooooooooaaaaaaaaaaaaaaaa aaaaaaaaaaaaaaaaaaaaaaaaaaaaaaaaaaaaaaaaaaaaaaaaaaaaaaaaa???!!!"

A rush.

A vortex of power, seeping in through every pore, collecting at the center of his body. The quantity was too much to reside fully within a human body. It was the same as how only a certain amount of air could fit into a balloon. If you tried to pack even more into it, the eventual outcome was clear.

Red blood sprayed out from his arms and legs.

He felt like sparks were arcing across his spine and neck.

His blood vessels and nerves weren't safe, either. He now knew the feeling of all that wiring, split up into countless branches, splitting and tearing apart. His two legs shook madly, and his body, which had been so sturdy before, was now on the verge of breaking.

But he wouldn't fall.

The sword he had driven into the ground—and his own heart. Steadying himself with only those two things, this man would never crumple.

The damage didn't stay in his physical body.

Something important, something that had maintained his functioning as a sorcerer, continued to pull apart.

He was a saint—and a member of God's Right Seat. A fusion of the two talents was within him, and he was one of only a very few sorcerers who wielded such immense power. He could feel the wellspring of that power shattering, crumbling to pieces. Even now, with every passing moment, more of his magical power was lost. He would probably drain himself of it utterly. And it was likely things wouldn't stop there. Even as he felt himself breaking apart from within, he didn't stop.

The enemy's strength would weaken for every bit of telesma that flowed to him.

The angelic power of salvation would decrease the chances his opponent would kill others.

That was enough.

As long as that held true, the man would be able to continue gritting his teeth and confront this incredible telesma.

And...

Roar!!!!!!

Accelerator's attack landed squarely on Misha Kreutzev.

The Eradication it had tried to rain upon them lost control over its aim, only causing the night sky to shake before stopping.

As Misha Kreutzev careened away, Accelerator and the angel of science headed toward it.

To deliver a follow-up attack.

To prevent it from further reducing the battlefield to scrap metal and rubble.

And...

Fiamma of the Right smiled slightly.

The total telesma Acqua of the Back had forced into its own body was around half of what Gabriel could muster. Even that alone was plenty threatening—but nevertheless, humans were humans. Unless he was a special exception like Sasha Kreutzev, he wouldn't be able to contain the entirety of an archangel.

And.

"Even fifty percent is more than enough to win," said Fiamma, sounding bored. "To have lost both your sainthood and your place in God's Right Seat, only for it to end now? Your life will go unrequited."

Kill them, he commanded.

That would be the end.

The archangel Misha Kreutzev would kill the angel of science and Academy City esper, then swiftly eliminate Academy City's armored units. None could stop Fiamma's plans. As long as he had Misha, even if over fifty thousand nuclear missiles were fired at the same time, they could never bring down the Star of Bethlehem.

That was how it should have been.

But she wasn't moving.

Misha Kreutzev, to whom he had given his command to kill, was frozen.

He had a bad feeling about this.

He had a perfectly advantageous position—and now it had very slightly tilted. It was no more than an extremely tiny movement, and yet, he felt an unease that he couldn't ignore, as though everything, strangely, was about to slip away.

And—

"That bastard…"

Fiamma of the Right figured it out.

One other thing.

There was one other presence that could only use his full power on this irregular battlefield.

"That bastard."

8

Meanwhile.

Touma Kamijou was in a corner of the Star of Bethlehem. At the ritual site on the fortress's rightmost section, where Misha Kreutzev's summoning using Sasha's body had been conducted.

Fiamma had apparently embedded the Index-remote-control Soul Arm into his staff in order to control Misha. If Kamijou could destroy that staff with his right hand, it should stop Misha, but to do that, he'd have to clash with Fiamma, an unknown value.

And there was one more thing.

Kamijou had thought of a possibility that could stop Misha Kreutzev with more certainty and also quicker.

"...Misha Kreutzev appeared after the Star of Bethlehem did," he murmured—as if to explain to Sasha next to him or perhaps to confirm it to himself. "If he could use something as strong as an archangel in the war, he didn't need to conserve it. He wouldn't have to cause World War III. He could have just done everything with the one archangel. But he didn't. Not until the Star of Bethlehem appeared.

"In other words," he continued, "he needed the Star of Bethlehem to summon the archangel Misha Kreutzev and control it!! He couldn't have used it before the fortress went airborne, even if he wanted to!! There's something in the Star propping up Misha. If I can find whatever it is and destroy it with my right hand, then...!!"

Touma Kamijou had grabbed onto a thin pillar-like object in the ritual site.

It was about three centimeters across. There were dozens of straight-standing pillars with black fluid flowing through them. Others had white fluid in them, too. According to Sasha, white and black formed a pair, controlling the ritual site's "gate," used for drawing occult powers from outside to inside. There were dozens of them because, apparently, that "power" needed complex routes to travel through.

There they were, right in front of him.

So he began to break every single one.

With shrill cracks and creaks and crashes, the transparent vessels shattered. The white-and-black liquid inside them spilled out, marbling together on the floor.

He felt something abruptly tilt.

He couldn't see it with his eyes, but it was something that was clearly there. And Touma Kamijou had definitely just felt its foundation shake.

*   *   *

And.

With Acqua of the Back reducing its total power by half.

And Touma Kamijou destroying the foundation supporting it.

As the strongest Level Five created by Academy City and the angel of science fiercely attacked, Misha Kreutzev...

The archangel's roar ripped through the night sky over Russia.

A scream filled with sinister emotion, utterly incomprehensible to the human mind but clearly different from the simple sound of an explosion.

Misha's form, barely maintained in the shape of a human body, collapsed into a mush.

It reverted to a ball of pure power.

To an immense amount of energy.

And it was a bomb.

Accelerator, confronting the archangel from the closest position, gave a start; then, ignoring his electrode usage time, shot straight toward the archangel at full power.

...Doesn't matter if it's out of place, or incongruous, or whatever.

The power to press forward.

The power he never had when he'd been wandering around Russia after fleeing Academy City.

He detonated all of it.

Yeah, that's right!! I want to protect her! I don't want to lose her!! I don't even want to think about that!! If I can protect that one illusion, I'll face whatever reality I have to!!

He couldn't control that massive power with simple reflection alone.

He didn't know if the angel of science was an ally or an enemy, but he shouted this at her:

"Hold it baaaaaaaaaaaaaaaaaaaaaaaaaaaaaaaaaaaaaaaaaaaaaaaaaaaaa aaaaaaaaaaaaaaaaaaaaaaaaaaaaaaaaaaaaaaaaaaaaaaaaaaaaaaaaack!!!!!!"

Did she have time to move?
Was she able to make it?
Immediately after.

It detonated.

A pure-white flash of light reached out, shaped like a dome. A terrifying light, all too pure, that swallowed everything. Light intense enough to burn one's eyes even if they were shut painted over the unnatural night in bright white.

Normally, everything for dozens of miles around would have gone to ash.

It was an explosion due to a unique force. Even aside from that, if odd side effects occurred, it wouldn't be strange. It was even highly likely it would have become a literal barren wasteland.

However.

Before the explosion could expand, it gave off unnatural distortions.

The angel of science rammed the massive power residing in her body into Accelerator, who then manipulated its vectors to create a transparent wall that surrounded the explosion in a spherical shape. The explosion had reached out about three hundred meters in the span of an instant and, covering it completely with an outer shell, too, further increased the force trying to tear through it from the inside.

Light and sound intensified.

But Accelerator held it back.

Two enormous powers contended, one from within and the other from without.

The entire event only took place over a few seconds.

And then…

After verifying the telesma's dispersion, Acqua's hand slowly released his giant sword.

The hand was covered in blood. No—his hand was not the only thing stained red.

He could feel his power draining.

Leaving his sword, stuck halfway into the ground, Acqua collapsed onto the snow, his face not changing very much. His mouth alone, however, had just slightly slackened.

This was enough.

If they could just eliminate the archangel Gabriel, the war's balance would shift greatly. Fiamma possessed a great strength, but he was too confident in it. That was why he'd forgotten people could challenge strong enemies by banding together. He could no longer see the option of entrusting the war to another with the same goals. Indeed—just like Acqua himself was, once upon a time.

His nerves and blood vessels had been torn asunder, and he had lost his foundation for controlling magic.

His life wouldn't last much longer, either.

He would die, taking the archangel with him.

This was enough.

It wasn't his goal to see this through to the end. He had prepared one necessary foundation for that purpose. With this, everyone had taken another step closer to Fiamma high in the sky. So it didn't matter. As long as everyone was smiling in the distant future, it was a grand enough victory for a mercenary like himself. Whether he was part of that future wasn't the problem.

Then it happened.

"Damn it…!!"

He heard a voice. He saw someone running through the snow to him. A young man. Asian. If he recalled correctly—one of the people using that Russian anti-air gun in an attempt to defend that settlement from the foreign mercenary unit.

"What happened? Those aren't just any gunshot wounds. What happened, damn it?! We're already busy with the Steam Dispenser stuff!! Hey, Takitsubo, I don't know much about first aid. Can you do something?!"

The pair squatted down next to Acqua and took out what appeared to be bandages. However, Acqua's expression never changed. He knew his own body.

"Don't…bother," he said, working his mouth that was filled with the taste of blood. "In any case, I will not last long. This is a battlefield. There will be no lack of need for medical supplies. Find someone else or consider the future and set it aside for that. Either way, there is no reason to waste it now."

"Shut up."

"I cannot reveal the details, but I just picked a fight with the man behind this entire war. I succeeded in frustrating his plans for now, but I cannot deny the possibility of a follow-up attack. It's dangerous to be here. Leave me and go."

"Didn't you hear what I just fucking said?! If that's the case, I definitely can't leave you!! I'm so sick of this already!! I'm not gonna watch anyone else die in front of me!!"

"I've fulfilled my objective. I am nothing but a hindrance now."

"Then…what about the people waiting for you?" squeezed out Hamazura.

Acqua's motions paused for a moment.

Hamazura continued, "That's how you've lived your life until now, right? When you helped Digurv and me and the others, it wasn't because we were special to you. That's just how you've lived up till now!! Someone like that could never be alone. Even if you don't think about it, you have a lot of people behind you. What about all those people, huh?!"

It was a strength that didn't exist in Acqua.

Because of that, he looked steadily at this man named Shiage Hamazura.

Each one of his words was like a wedge.

A wedge to stop his body as it continued to slide down the road to death.

Hamazura's words were certainly not simple salvation.

In fact, the force with which he drove them in actually gave him pain.

However.

Those words just barely held Acqua together.

"You died protecting the world. You fell defending others. Do you think they'll be happy with any of that stuff?! Of course not!! Was your whole reason for fighting to watch those waiting for you cry while you put smiles on other people's faces?! I don't think so!!"

What came to his mind then, with all the blood lost and his consciousness hazy, was that self-satisfied Knight Leader, the old man from the Astrologers' Brigade, and the couple threatened by the Knights of Orleans.

And.

The third princess of Britain.

"...Stand up, hero."

Not even caring anymore that he was wounded to the verge of death, Hamazura grabbed Acqua by the collar.

He grabbed him and said this:

"Staaaaaaaaaaaaaaaaaaaaaaaaaaaaaaand uuuuuuuuuuuuuuuuuuu uuuuuuuuuuuuuuuuuuuuuuuuuuuuuuuuuuuuuuuuuuuuuuuuuuuuup!!!!!!"

There was a *whmmp*.

It was the sound of Acqua, who had fallen faceup, grabbing onto the snowy land with his hand.

He could hear a pulse.

He was still alive.

This wasn't the end.

If he could still move...

"Ooooooooooooooooooooooooooooooooooooooooooooooooooooooooo oooooooooooooooooooooooooooooooooooooooooooooooooooooooooooo oooooooooooooooooooooooooooooooooooooooooooooooooooooooooh!!"

Even as his body audibly creaked and cracked, even as still more fresh red blood spurted from him, Acqua of the Back stood up once again.

His power as a saint had been lost.

Nor could he use his power as one of God's Right Seat.

His body had been torn apart and reduced to that of any other normal person, Acqua nevertheless gritted his teeth and began to temper mana inside him again. He allocated that power only to controlling his physical body, trying to keep any more blood from seeping out of his wounds.

He barely had any strength left.

He probably couldn't even heft that sword, taller than he was, that he'd brought with him as his weapon all this time.

But.

So what?

The title of true hero wasn't for people who gave up after falling down one time.

It was for those who got back up, again and again, in response to the people's cries.

9

"I see."

Fiamma of the Right picked up his staff.

The staff with the Index-remote-controlling Soul Arm affixed to the top, which he used to control the archangel.

Gabriel had apparently headed for the surface in pursuit of the parchment, but she had failed to retrieve it. That parchment had all the necessary information for Project Bethlehem.

But it wasn't an issue.

Fiamma's and Gabriel's senses were linked. And Gabriel's perception capabilities were far greater than that of humans. Even if the parchment was tucked away in the target's pocket, he could obtain the magical info written on it.

He'd already gotten the knowledge he needed.

Fiamma had extremely deep knowledge regarding Michael. And after gleaning the necessary knowledge from the 103,000 grimoires, he could clear away the rest of the obstacles in his way, too.

But there was one thing that even he didn't have.

The other archangels aside from Michael—in other words, the symbols of the other members of God's Right Seat.

The most secret of secrets in the Russian Church, that has reorganized unconfirmed information collected from all over Russia and inferred spells for each angel. If I can obtain that, I will have no problems left.

He didn't need this staff anymore.

He removed the Soul Arm for controlling Index attached to the top.

"I see, I see, I see."

He twirled the staff around.

Then smiled pleasantly and said:

"Damn you, you filthy piece of shit."

Crack.

He broke the staff in two.

After tossing the scraps aside, Fiamma smoothly held out his right hand. He had a rough position. He held his palm in that direction, then muttered something under his breath.

Sound vanished.

An intense flash of light burst forth.

It crushed and melted the walls of the Star of Bethlehem in one hit, then blew away several buildings as well, charging in a straight line toward its target.

He didn't get any feedback.

And if he'd gotten too much, that would have been a problem anyway.

After all, it had probably been repelled by the right arm in question.

Fiamma heard a strange crackling noise from around his right shoulder. His third arm, which had disintegrated before, was on the verge of separating. But for Fiamma, now bolstered by the knowledge in the 103,000 volumes, it didn't present much of an obstacle.

Tap.

He took just one step forward.

And with only that, Fiamma's body traveled over five kilometers. Even if there was no floor along the way, even if it was through the very air, it didn't matter. If there was an open, level route, he could move as far as he wanted.

He arrived in a room.

It was the ritual site where he'd called the archangel using Sasha Kreutzev's body. His earlier attack had caused over half the room to collapse, and most of its interior furnishings had been dropped onto a lower level as though something had dragged them down there. The boy he was looking for stood alone at the ritual site. He also spotted something red in the hole leading to the lower layer. Maybe someone had fallen into it, trapped by the collapse.

"You seem to enjoy causing me trouble," said Fiamma—one hand toying with the Soul Arm used for remotely controlling Index. "Thanks to you, I had to execute the ritual before Academy City or Britain could interfere. Which means I'll be taking that right arm of yours now."

"…You think it'll go that easy? You don't have Misha anymore. I still don't know why things went so well, but humans managed to beat an archangel. No matter how you think about it, the scales are tipping in our favor."

"That doesn't warrant any worry on my part," said Fiamma, pointing to the sky.

The building's walls and ceiling had been blown up by his attack. Thanks to that, the unnatural night sky beyond the collapsed structural material was visible.

Yes.

The spiky-haired boy must have realized.

That even though the archangel Misha Kreutzev had been defeated, the sky hadn't changed at all—and why that was significant.

"The angel's role ended after it changed the night sky to my liking," described Fiamma—while spreading his third arm out farther.

"I talked about how the symbols of Uriel and Raphael were shifted, out of place, right? And how Misha Kreutzev's name originates in *Michael*—and how it is unfit to name itself Gabriel."

The spiky-haired boy seemed to be on his guard, but it was too late.

Now that Fiamma was talking about it, it was over.

"I lifted only the Star of Bethlehem into the incomplete skies filled with telesma after erasing all stars from the sky using Gabriel as part of a ceremony to regulate a great flow of power and reset the four aspects...You defeated the magic circle that Misha covered a portion of the sky with during Angel Fall, as well as the Croce di Pietro, which used the positions of the stars as seen from earth. I don't need to explain to you how crucial the magical meaning is that comes with the idea of controlling the skies like a screen. To begin with, the prophet knew of Jesus's birth by the appearance of a *certain star* in the sky. The large-scale spell I'm using essentially applies that legendary truth.

"Still, I also affected the flow of power on the surface by moderately destroying churches and temples all over the world, too," added Fiamma.

Heaven and earth.

Three and four.

In other words, he now had exclusive possession of all numbers crucial to Crossist culture.

"What...? What are you trying...to...?"

"I'll ask you instead. You didn't think this would be over just because the Star of Bethlehem had risen, did you?" jeered Fiamma. "You know how it is. I'm just saying I have to prepare the location properly before I can execute the spell I want. Phase one is just about over, but despite how early it is, there's a nice little bonus in store."

Ker-crack!! went a strange noise.

A starry sky spread out.

First was yellow, then red, then blue, and finally green. Oddly colored stars began spreading across the pitch-black night sky, as if putting a veil over it, all in time to Fiamma's signal.

The Star of Bethlehem was a gargantuan planetarium.

"Did you know this little tidbit?"

A starry sky of colors absolutely impossible in nature. An amateur with no knowledge of sorcery would never be able to decipher the detailed meaning behind it. But somewhere, deep inside his very life force, he understood. Understood this clear, true world. Understood the feeling of the four aspects returning to their original locations.

"Fire, water, wind, and earth—each one of these four aspects holds up the edge of its respective power, but at the same time, manipulating one aspect affects, in a broad sense, all the other aspects as well. That's why in large-scale rituals, excluding realistic combat actions, it's fundamental to ready not one symbolic weapon, but the entire set. Even if that ritual is of fire. In other words, the ability to control all four aspects rested within my fire from the beginning. I should have gained magnificent power by controlling them all…If only a distortion hadn't existed in those aspects worldwide."

To which Fiamma explained:

"One can only fully wield true power in a true world."

Boom!!!!!! Something invisible exploded out of his body.

It was intent to kill.

A force overwhelming enough to make Kamijou feel like he was on pins and needles.

"…"

But he had no reason to back off.

The man in front of him was holding the Soul Arm that could remotely control Index. To destroy that, he'd have to defeat the root cause of this aura.

Kamijou clenched his right hand into a tight fist.

His mind naturally drew toward Fiamma's right shoulder.

To the third arm.

Writhing.

Something massive, some power that should have caused it to disintegrate, was gathering in it.

"It's time I showed you the meaning of true power."

COMBAT REPORT

Mikoto was sitting wearily on a snowfield in Russia.

As she did, the Sister spoke to her, saying, "Have you calmed down? asks Misaka."

"Yeah…Sorry about that. Could you explain this to me again?"

"Nu-AD1967. Launch preparations for an old Soviet strategic nuclear warhead are currently underway, says Misaka, summarizing her report."

"Okay, wait. Wait a second. A nuclear warhead—a nuke? You mean the president of Russia gave the go-ahead on it?"

As Mikoto blanched, the Sister's face remained expressionless. She tilted her head slightly.

"No conversations regarding adjustments are occurring on normal military channels, says Misaka, confirming with herself. In addition, there are no visible signs of wireless transmissions of nuclear launch codes, supplements Misaka. This is only a speculation, but I believe this is an act by an independent group led by a man named Nikolai Tolstoj."

"What's that mean…?" Mikoto frowned. "You're telling me a Russian unit loaded a nuclear warhead into a missile without asking? But they wouldn't be able to detonate it without the launch codes from their leader, right?"

If it didn't work that way, they ran the risk of any old soldier with dangerous ideas pulling the trigger on the extinction of humanity. This nation had many missiles and several launch facilities; their security for it should have been airtight.

"Not necessarily, says Misaka, listening in on the communications with a troubled face."

"You haven't batted an eye."

"It seems the independent unit plans to use an exchange warhead, answers Misaka in mild annoyance." The Sister shook her head. "Have you heard the story that right after the Cold War between east and west ended, several nuclear warheads and radioactive materials flowed out of Russia, whose infrastructure had collapsed at the time? asks Misaka for confirmation."

"Well, I guess I've heard the story before, but…not how much is truth and how much is just an urban legend."

"Then what about how a large number of nuclear scientists and technical information left the country at the same time?"

"…"

"These warheads were traded with the purpose of using them, but most of them would have been actually impossible to detonate because of the lack of authentication codes, says Misaka. But exceptions exist for certain missiles. Nuclear missile security locks are set into an outer shell surrounding the nuclear matter, explains Misaka. In other words—"

"If they take out the insides, then put that into a new outer shell they created…"

"They would be able to detonate the nuclear matter, concludes Misaka. And with precisely the same power, adds Misaka."

The Sister spoke fluidly.

It seemed like more information than she could get just by listening in on those military communications just now. Maybe she was getting intel in real time by using the Misaka network.

"After the Soviet Union collapsed, these exchange warheads cropped up in manufacturing projects at multiple sites, mainly ones with the aim of gaining independence from Russia—but when Russia's national power recovered, they began a special military operation to aggressively hunt them down, allegedly to take responsibility for their own nukes and contribute to world peace, explains Misaka. In official records, these exchange warheads were dismantled and their densities lowered before they used them as fuel for nuclear reactors."

"But the independent team actually saved all the ones they recovered? As nuclear weapons they could fire whenever they wanted, without the president's permission?"

"They seem to have prepared vehicular launchers in order to fire an exchange warhead using the Nu-AD1967 at that fortress up in the sky, says Misaka, revealing their plans."

"You're kidding, right...?" murmured Mikoto.

No matter how incomprehensible that fortress was, and no matter how many times the man on it had returned alive from deadly battlefields, it would be horrific if anything like that detonated there.

And the damage wouldn't stop there, either.

If that strange fortress had some sort of crazy defensive system that could even withstand nuclear explosions, it still wouldn't end on a happy note.

The issue was the altitude of the fortress they were targeting.

"...Wasn't America or someone researching safer, smaller-scale nuclear warheads?"

"Are you referring to the project of developing nuclear weapons with destructive scope ranges from three to five kilometers across, which would allow them to deploy nuclear weapons while also avoiding spreading the fallout into the sky? confirms Misaka. Misaka believes those were designed for destroying underground facilities."

Right.

Even during the overheated nuclear arms race during the Cold War, there was a taboo: to restrict the ensuing fallout to below certain altitudes. It was so taboo that instead of creating one giant bomb, they created a warhead called a MIRV that would basically launch an entire rain of little nuclear bombs.

What was the reason for not spreading the fallout above a certain altitude?

What was so concerning that the great powers, who were considering even full-blown nuclear war, would nevertheless restrain themselves to absolute avoidance of doing so?

"This is a lot worse than *awful*...If they fire a nuclear weapon at a target so high up...!!"

"Based on the Nu-AD1967's explosion magnitude, there is an extremely high probability that the fallout produced by attacking the floating fortress will not end in the skies, but rather be engulfed into layers of airflow, thus polluting the entire planet, says Misaka, reporting on the network's simulated result. It is predicted that the radioactive matter will adversely affect life, and the fallout will block out the sunlight, drastically altering Earth's environment and causing intense food shortages due to poor plant growth conditions, says Misaka with concern."

The risk of fallout always existed, even for nuclear explosions that carried over the surface.

If one to ten thousand meters were added onto that, the level of resulting fallout would be immeasurable.

"You said they were preparing a mobile launcher, right? Do you know exactly where it is?"

"A rough position, yes. But in order to avoid damage from the nuclear explosion, they are trying to fire the missile from a spot over seventy kilometers from our current location, adds Misaka."

"Hmm."

Mikoto looked around, then gestured with her jaw to one place.

It was a group of Academy City vehicles. Many tanks and armored cars, transporting several powered suits, were even now on the move and firing their artillery.

"...Let's just steal one of them or something. You know how to drive a car?"

St. George's Cathedral.

Stiyl Magnus was running through its basement. Not through a room somewhere—through a long passage made of stone. St.

George's Cathedral had escape routes that went on for miles, centered on the building, like a spiderweb. Real ones, fake ones, trapped ones, detours for getting surrounded in the passages, and so on—their uses and importance were many and varied.

Footsteps were approaching from behind.

Strange footsteps. The number of them didn't match the distance.

I can't afford to keep running forever.

Stiyl ground his teeth.

If I give her calculation abilities any room to breathe, that by itself gives Fiamma an easy way to use her!!

A moment later.

"Chapter fifteen, verse four. Cutting off hostile's escape route and commencing certain disposition."

Wh-whmm!! The entire space around them shook.

By the time he'd noticed it, the underground passage in front of Stiyl collapsed as though crushed by the hand of a giant.

Stiyl whipped back around.

Two eyes, shining, deep in the darkness.

Three more white lights hovered near Index as well.

"Chapter seventeen, verse thirty-three. Confirmed distinctive Norse mythology features from hostile. Replicating the sword of the god of fertility as a countermeasure. Immediately executing."

Vwoom!! The three white lights shot forth.

"Gah!!"

Stiyl produced a sword of flames right away, but the three lights suddenly switched from their straight-line trajectories to moving like slippery, living creatures, worming their way around Stiyl's sword of flames.

Freyr's sword…?!

Weapons that freely danced in the air and ended enemies' lives without fail appeared often in many myths around the world, not just Norse mythology. The sword of Freyr, god of fertility, was a perfect example. The legend went that if someone wise possessed it, it would fight on its own, bringing absolute victory to its owner.

In ancient Norse religion, both gods and humans could possibly be defeated or die. Nevertheless, in all the legends, not one had ever depicted Freyr's sword losing.

It was that level of myth.

That level of destructive power.

They went through the gaps in his defense—his sword of flames—and Stiyl, with the swords' tips now pointed at his throat, shouted:

"Innocentius!!"

He no longer cared about the damage to himself.

A fiery titan appeared a moment later, parrying the three floating swords even as the burst of hot wind blew Stiyl, its user, directly backward.

His back collided with the collapsed wall blocking the passage.

A tiny bit of spare time.

But that wouldn't be enough to turn it around.

"Chapter twenty, verse nine. Distorted Crossist motif confirmed. Beginning construction of optimal spell for use against the aforementioned spell. Activation preparations complete for spell name Eli Eli Lema Sabachthani. Executing at once."

A giant magic circle appeared in midair, centered on Index's face, and from it fired dark-red rays of light.

They easily tore Innocentius apart, dispersed it, shot right past Stiyl, and gouged a huge hole in the mountain of debris.

"…I see," said Stiyl, putting a hand on the wall and barely managing to stand up on his own two feet. "I'm up against the 103,000 grimoires. It only makes sense a mere single Innocentius couldn't compete with it.

"However," he added.

"I never said I only had one trump card."

Boom!! came an explosion.

Next to Stiyl was a fiery titan.

But not just on one side of him.

One Innocentius now reigned at both his right and left.

"Double."

For a short time, Index closely observed the phenomenon.

Eventually, eyes still emotionless, she spoke.

"Chapter twenty-one, verse forty-four. Commencing construction of countermeasure against multiple targets. Executing—"

And then it happened.

"Triple."

Boom!! Another burst went off.

Index's words stopped abruptly. It seemed to be considering whether the command she was about to execute would obstruct her.

Stiyl knew he had expended a large amount of mana—and thus the life force it was created from. But even as the greasy sweat broke out, he grinned.

"You didn't think…that I'd leave my abilities to rot after feeling so powerless back then, did you?"

Of course, Stiyl couldn't always use three Innocentiuses with his power alone. No matter how new the spell designs, there was a line that you couldn't cross on just your own strength. And Stiyl hadn't yet overcome that wall.

Instead, he made up for what he lacked with the Soul Arms in St. George's Cathedral.

He'd been running away this entire time so he could find the items he needed, retrieve them, and use them.

But the library of grimoires didn't stop.

She continued her purely methodical analysis.

"Chapter twenty-three, verse eleven. Confirmed three-in-one structure. Identified target spell as serving a single role as three, aiming to conserve mana expenditure by circulating mana between three bodies."

Voom!! Served by her three swords of the fertility god around her, backed by her protruding bloodred wings, and eyes glittering with the eerie light of magic circles within them, Index said:

"There is but one countermeasure. Concluding that a focused attack on one of the three will cause the three-in-one structure to collapse."

*   *   *

They'd found it.

After parting with Acqua and going farther through the snowfield, Hamazura and Takitsubo were now hidden behind some conifer trunks, only their heads poking out so they could keep watch on a spot a short distance away. About fifty meters from them was a slightly moving figure. It was a soldier, dressed in a white combat uniform, slightly different in design from normal military uniforms, and armed with an assault rifle.

He seemed to be a lookout.

Farther ahead was the foot of a small mountain. Three large tanker trucks were parked there. Several other smaller vehicles were gathered there, too. Nearby, several men were carrying out some sort of work, even now.

There was an object that looked like a pole, about five meters high.

More than one, in fact. The men had put over ten poles in the ground, evenly separated, and now they were about to connect big hoses coming from the tankers to them.

"Is that the Steam Dispenser...?" murmured Hamazura, still hidden.

Next to him, Takitsubo nodded. "The tankers might be for the heat-retaining gel. I wonder if those poles are atomizers."

The soldier on lookout turned his head their way; Hamazura and Takitsubo quickly pulled their heads back behind the trees.

Hamazura took out his cell phone and contacted Grickin.

If they could just figure out the conditions regarding the settlement, the Steam Dispenser, and the wind direction, he could calculate where they should flee.

However.

If this unit actually sprayed the stuff, nothing guaranteed that he'd be able to keep casualties to zero.

After hanging up and observing what was in front of them, he saw that almost ten lookouts had spread out, essentially in a giant circle with the work site at the foot of the mountain in the center. They seemed to be slowly patrolling a certain area rather than standing still in one place. Even so, Hamazura and Takitsubo wouldn't be able to slip past them to get close to the tankers in the middle. If they did worm through a blind spot and move in, the lookouts were sure to spot their footprints in the snow after circling back on their patrol routes.

Hamazura became ever more conscious of the assault rifle, now cold, in his hands.

...*Can't win with this much of a numbers difference. And besides, they're pro soldiers. I couldn't even do anything in a one-on-one shoot-out. Once the first gunshot goes off, it's all over.*

But they didn't have time to stand here watching in silence. Preparations to spray the bacteriological weapon were continuing, sure and steady, even now. The end of those preparations would come with them going with the absolute worst choice. He had to finish things before that happened.

Despite the freezing blizzard, Hamazura was sweating nervously— but then Takitsubo said something unexpected.

"...Hamazura, we should wait for them to leave."

"What?"

Hamazura frowned. At this rate, the Russian agents would use the bioweapon. And if that happened, the settlement where Digurv and the others were was done for...

"Hamazura, the report said something. The bacteria wall used by the Kremlin Report is the kind that spreads through the air. It can get into your body not only through your lungs, but your skin, too. It also breaks down oils, and since it will create holes in the filters used for masks and ducts for biochemical weapons, no standard defensive measures will work."

"So what? Isn't that exactly why we have to prevent them from spraying something that dangerous?" asked Hamazura.

Takitsubo pointed to the team of agents still doing their work on the white snowfield. "How are they going to escape the bacteria?"

"Huh...?"

"Masks and thick suits won't work. Even if they climb inside a cutting-edge tank, it's no use. So as soon as the soldiers deploy the curtain of bacteria, it'll get them, too."

Now that she mentioned it, that was true.

And when he looked at them again, he saw that the lookout soldiers weren't wearing any kind of crazy masks—despite handling a dangerous bioweapon.

"Hamazura. I think they'll set it on a timer. Once they set up the Steam Dispenser and the bacteria, they'll hurry to get somewhere safe. They have to, since you can't rely on masks or suits. But if they do…"

"I get it. We don't have to fight them recklessly. There will be some time after the team leaves but before the timer hits zero. If we use that time to get near the Steam Dispenser and disable it, we can stop the weapon from activating!!"

"But the window to make our attempt probably won't be that long. The team will probably set the time limit to deploy the bacteria wall as quickly as possible while still assuring their own safety. And with a machine that large, I doubt we have time to destroy the whole thing. We should probably look for a weak spot."

Their on-hand weapons consisted of a handgun and an assault rifle. Not suitable for blowing anything up. The fuel tanks of the tankers and other vehicles were probably filled with gasoline, so if they were going to use anything, it would probably need to be that.

The device's broad construction comprised almost ten Steam Dispenser poles and three tank trucks. Several of the slender vehicles apart from that would be for the work as well.

Frankly speaking, it would be easy to use those fuel tanks to blow up one or two of them.

But the flames, smoke, and heat produced from that would hinder them from doing any further work. The heated winds would be like a wall; even if they didn't enter the fire zone directly, one shift in the wind direction, and they'd be burned to a crisp, from skin to lungs. To make sure they blew up all the vehicles serving as part of the mechanism, they would need calculations on the level of building deconstruction work. Obviously, they didn't have that sort of free time right now.

A weak point, then.

If they could find one weak point, like Takitsubo said, something that would stop the entire device when destroyed by itself, they'd be able to avoid this sort of problem.

Hamazura narrowed his eyes, staring past the blizzard, then eventually murmured, "...There's a generator car."

"?"

"The armored car to the right of the tankers. See those thick power cables going to it? There's gotta be a generator inside there. Kinuhata once made me watch a military C movie, and in one part of it, they were saying how they were making progress on getting recent military supplies to run on electricity, starting with targeting devices. It'd apparently be useful for a lot of stuff, like night vision or getting help from UAVs, but they said the problem was that the battery would drain really frequently. So then they needed to set up charging stations in the desert, or jungle, or wherever the battlefield was."

"But it's an armored car on the outside. We won't be able to blow it up so easily. It might be a different story if we can get inside it, but if the team locks the hatch before they leave, we won't be able to pry it open, will we...?"

"We don't need to blow it up."

Hamazura lowered himself to Takitsubo's height, then directed her gaze to the armored car's rear.

"You see those three exhaust pipes sticking out right above the generator car's rear end? That's too many just for an armored car engine. I think maybe its core is a diesel generator. Our goal is to stop electricity from getting sent to the entire Steam Dispenser setup from the generator car. All we have to do is stop that generator."

"?"

"Doesn't matter if it's gasoline or diesel, or a car engine or a generator—they basically all work the same on the inside. If you stuff dirt or something into an internal combustion engine's exhaust pipe, it'll break down. Anti-Skill was starting to use these gel bazooka things so they could force runaway cars' engines to stall."

"What if it's all a giant lithium-ion battery?"

"Then we'll cut through all the cables coming from the generator car. I'd be afraid of getting electrocuted, though, so I'd want to avoid that if possible."

Then Takitsubo's small hand tugged on his clothes.

There was movement among the working team through the blizzard. They'd been hurriedly running back and forth through the installment before, but now, after contacting someone else on a radio, they were getting into small vehicles, one after another.

"Hamazura."

"I got it."

Once the team left the site, they'd quickly approach the Steam Dispenser devices and launch an attack on the generator car's exhaust pipes. There was little time. In the worst case, the time limit might be over within minutes. Not knowing precisely how much time was left exacerbated their impatience.

But that didn't mean they could afford to mess up now.

They couldn't beat those soldiers in a fight. Which meant they couldn't afford to be spotted. They had to prevent them from getting even a glimpse until they'd completely left the area.

Hamazura and Takitsubo kept themselves low in the trees and held their breath.

…Will this work? thought Hamazura, aware of his own pulse more than he needed to be.

They already knew the lengths to which these soldiers would go. He couldn't discount the possibility they'd set up land mines or something around here, either. He'd learned they'd use cowardly traps like that openly back in Digurv's settlement.

The sounds of several engines starting up overlapped.

The team was about to leave.

He would know if there were traps if he followed the cars' movements. At the very least, they wouldn't be dumb enough to set up land mines along the route they took. Still hunched over, Hamazura peeled his eyes and focused his mind. He didn't know how long the car tracks would remain in this blizzard. He would have to fully memorize the safe route.

And then.

Something happened that he hadn't expected.

Baaaang!! A gunshot rang out.

The snow right next to Hamazura leaped. When he realized a rifle bullet had struck that spot, he crouched down in a panic. But he didn't make it. He knew far too well what situation they were in now.

"Shit. They noticed us!!"

The vehicles about to leave the area suddenly hit the brakes. Several doors opened, and heavily armed soldiers came pouring out. He knew from the start he couldn't pull off a win against them. In a straight-up shoot-out, both in quantity and quality, Hamazura and Takitsubo were at a severe disadvantage.

In that instant, the only plan he could immediately come up with was this:

No matter what, he had to get Takitsubo out of here.

Removing the safety on the assault rifle in his hands, trying desperately to control his unconsciously shallow breathing, he steeled his resolve.

But what exactly would he do?

Sweat crept down the hand holding the grip. An awful blank came into his head. And as he stood there in incredible tension, he heard a high-pitched whistling.

He looked straight up.

In the sky—something slowly flying.

An Academy City...supersonic bomber?!

An extremely large machine, over eighty meters long. Hamazura didn't have time to think any more about the monstrous aircraft ripping through the air.

A moment later, there was an explosion.

It wasn't simply bombs dropping.

He only realized quite a bit later that they'd used magnetism or something to accelerate and fire shells, which had then crashed into the ground at over the speed of sound.

Grahhhhh!!!!!! The incredible bursting noise enveloped Hamazura's entire body.

The Steam Dispensers and related vehicles set up on the foot of the mountain all disappeared into a sea of fire. Despite being a good distance away, the agents' getaway vehicles were sent flipping over as well. Even Hamazura and Takitsubo ended up buried in the snow.

On the ground, Hamazura found a radio right nearby, possibly one that was blasted over by the explosion. It must have belonged to one of the people on the team.

He heard a voice from it.

A Japanese voice.

"Yo. I know someone's down there from the magnetic readings. If you're a kindhearted volunteer, let's shake hands. I'm basically one myself."

"Gahhh, damn, Academy City...?"

Hamazura felt like something was wrong.

If he could hear the void from a Russian radio, the person was using a frequency anyone could hear, regardless of enemy or ally. That didn't seem like how Academy City's "dark side" did something.

Which meant...

They're from...Academy City like us...but they're not...from the underworld...? Is this guy a regular soldier...A teacher, maybe...?

"That's right. Dear Ekalielya and the others who invaded the Sea of Japan let me through. And now I can do all this charity work. It's been rough telling the difference between fighter aircraft and attack aircraft lately— What I'm trying to say is I've got a ton of work to do."

That moment.

A strange chemical reaction occurred in Shiage Hamazura's mental state.

He was on the run from Academy City. He was happy reinforcements had come, but if they chased him around with a monster of a plane like that, things would be hopeless.

On the other hand, though, he was still relieved enough to let his body fully relax. Things really hadn't been normal until now. Some street thug standing up to privateers and Russian military teams was stranger than anything else.

Without a care for Hamazura as he thought those things, the monstrous aircraft turned sharply in the air, coming back around again. It fired a large amount of bombs with magnetic force along its flight path, spreading explosive flames in a straight line on the surface.

Light.

Sound.

They were intense enough that Hamazura, some distance away, had to cover his face. But he could somehow feel the energy draining from his body. His muscles, tightened past where they needed to be, began to unwind.

Maybe we're saved.

The fact that one who was supposed to protect the peace could protect them from this senseless violence.

It made Hamazura feel a natural peace and relief, even though after this, that monstrous airplane could start gunning for them.

Maybe we won't have to get killed by that insane bioweapon, and maybe Digurv's settlement can escape danger, too...

What was the man thinking right now?

Did he believe things were over now? Did he not know who exactly he was, having honed in on his position using only magnetic reactions?

And then another problem came up.

That was...

"Hey, is this—? Is this okay? The bioweapon is a lethal virus or something, isn't it?"

"That's why I'm making sure to torch every last bit of it. Get down and shut your eyes for a sec—and cover your ears and open your mouth. These bombs are white phosphorous-based, so they don't make too much noise, but that doesn't mean there won't be shock waves."

As expected, he had no time to object.

A second later, multiple bombs impacted on the Russian surface.

The bombs would have had considerable potential energy just by free-falling—but then magnetic force or something had accelerated them.

With an enormous shock wave, a crater appeared where the Steam Dispensers had been set up, and immediately after, the area transformed into a sea of fire. It was different from normal radiation—these flames were uncanny, spreading in more of a clinging way.

Within moments, the demonic device had been destroyed two, three times over.

The Russian agents didn't get away, either.

The bombing from the skies hadn't aimed directly for people. But the explosions' aftermath was brutal, swallowing them up. Many were flung up, then fell back onto the ground—after which they failed to move subsequently. They seemed to have been knocked out.

As if drawn by the explosive noises and shock waves, a large amount of snow collapsed on the mountain's slope. It was a good distance away from where Hamazura stood, but the snow that splashed upward after ramming into the ground immediately covered Hamazura and Takitsubo like the powder from a fire extinguisher.

His vision went to zero. Takitsubo should have been right next to him, and he couldn't even see her face. He truly couldn't even tell anymore that he was in a forested area.

"(…Takitsubo?! Where are you? Are you all right?!)"

Hamazura kept his voice down but still called out to his surroundings. He reached out with his hands, trying to grope around, but he felt only the sensation of hard tree trunks.

The Steam Dispensers, the bioweapon, the team of engineers—what had happened to them?

Confused and unable to see, Hamazura simply wandered.

How many minutes passed? Was it over ten?

When he was no longer able to even keep track of time, his hand grabbed something soft.

"Takitsubo!!"

Hastily, he embraced her, then looked at her face.

Yes, it was Rikou Takitsubo.

Black hair on the short side. Sleepy-looking eyes. Skin that was already pale but perhaps because of the cold—even protected by her clothes—seemed somewhat blue.

However.

"...Hama...zura..."

Rikou Takitsubo, who had been next to him just a second ago—did she always wear this lightweight yellow autumn coat? Was she wearing stockings that covered her legs? Was she always this tall? Was her voice always this deep?

"...Hamazura..."

Also.

Did the Takitsubo who Hamazura knew always laugh with such an evil expression?

"It's been so long, hasn't it, Haamazuraaaaaaaaaaaaaaaaaaaaaaaa?!"

Crackle-crackle-kreeeen!!!!!! Fissures began to appear from inside Takitsubo's face, made to look like a small animal. From inside, an entirely different woman's face peeked out.

A more violent one.

A more wicked one.

Features that gave a face to the very darkness of Academy City itself.

...She's...!!

A light purer than white formed in the back of one of her eyes.

As soon as it opened large enough to tear the corners of her eye, an intense bullet of light flew at Hamazura's face.

With all his strength, Hamazura threw his head to the side, and the fierce light and heat passed right by his ear. It knocked over conifer trees, launching upward, before slightly grazing the main wing of the Academy City supersonic fighter dominating the Russian skies. He glimpsed a long, thin box fire out of the out-of-control aircraft, but he couldn't take the time to turn his head that way.

The fourth-ranked Level Five.

Meltdown.

"Shizuri...Mugino...!!"

Hamazura shoved her away, then hastily tried to back off before his back knocked into a tree trunk.

What is she doing here?!

But there was no point in asking the question. When Hamazura looked at this woman's expression as she peeled off her special makeup and put her finger in her eye to wipe off the remnants of the melted false eye, he fully felt, whether he liked it or not, the vengefulness that could push all logic aside.

Where did Rikou Takitsubo go?

What should he do so the two of them could survive?

As he breathed rapidly, in and out, over and over, face-to-face with his impending mortal crisis, he thought:

I don't have a choice.

I'll have to settle things with this monster—with Shizuri Mugino.

AFTERWORD

To those of you who have purchased one book at a time, hello again.

To those of you who purchased the whole series at once, it's nice to meet you.

I'm Kazuma Kamachi.

Cut in half!! …You may be wondering why I say that so suddenly, but this time the idea is "cutting in half." To tell the truth, this point was originally planned to be where *A Certain Magical Index*, Vol. 21 turned from part one to part two. This same amount of pages actually would have been waiting for you after this…but my editor gave me some sage advice, saying "No can do. It'd get a bit too thick," and so we hurriedly cut it in half. This afterword, too, was something I tacked on with equal haste.

It may be due to the down-the-middle split, but for Volume 21, I feel as though that girl who showed up in Volume 4 ended up being the main feature. Even though a lot of characters clashed together in rapid succession, I got a little emotional when I thought about how far the people in this universe have come.

One runs toward the problem to resolve it, another still can't find any clues, and one is beaten into a chaotic hellscape. The protagonists have gotten themselves in a variety of situations, so please look forward to next time.

*   *   *

I'd like to thank my illustrator, Mr. Haimura, and my editor, Mr. Miki. With the war intensifying, I think the hurdles demanded on the illustration end have risen. Thank you for sticking with me again.

And a thanks goes out to my readers. It's a considerable number, twenty-three—but I was only able to keep piling them up because of you. I look forward to your continued support.

Now then, as I have you close the pages here,
and as I pray you will open the pages again next time,
here and now, I lay down my pen.

But Misha ain't the only archangel in this universe, heh.

Kazuma Kamachi